Dangerous Desires

By
D. L. Nolan

For permissions, contact: D. L. Nolan Smyrna, TN 37167 dnolan.creates@gmail.com

ISBNs First Edition, 2025:

Paperback: 979-8-90427-013-1

Hardcover: 979-8-90427-014-8

Cover design by Nicole P. Wolford

Dogman Photo is AI-generated

There are so many I would like to dedicate this book to. To my Sweetheart, who has been there for me time and time again. To my friends and family, who have encouraged me to chase my dream of becoming an author. To my amazing Beta Readers—your feedback, honesty, and support inspired me to keep going.

And last, but certainly not least—you, my readers. Thank you for taking a chance on a newbie. I can only hope you fall in love with my characters as much as I have.

This dedication is for all of you—past, present, and future readers. Thank you for joining my family of characters in Dangerous Desires

Pronunciation Guide:

Ashley — ASH-lee

Shana — SHAY-nuh (sometimes pronounced SHAH-nuh depending on region)

Aunt Ulla (Ursula) — AHNT OO-luh (short "oo" as in "book")

Mark — MARK

Wahaya — Wah-HIGH-yuh (Cherokee for "wolf" — emphasis on the middle syllable)

Finlay Alexander Stephenson (Alex) — FIN-lay AL-ex-AN-der STEE-ven-sun

Bidziil — BID-zeel (Navajo origin, meaning "strong")

Tsali — SAH-lee (the "T" is soft, almost silent — sounds like "SAH-lee") translation for Charlie. A Cherokee man who became a symbol of sacrifice and resistance during the 1830s Trail of Tears.

Adohi — Ah-DOH-hee (Cherokee for "tree" — emphasis on the second syllable)

Dusti Adeloquasti — DUH-stee Ah-day-loh-KWAH-stee (Cherokee-inspired — rhythmic, flowing pronunciation)

Richard Jackson Skullthorn — RICH-erd JACK-sun SKULL-thorn

Ihoki — Ee-HOH-kee — (a name of spiritual origin meaning "Sacred Heart" or "Beloved One")

Ahyoka — Ah-YOH-kah — Cherokee name meaning "She brought happiness

Content Advisory

This story is written with love. My characters are more than "just" characters in a book they have taken on a life of their own. As in life there are a few things that you might want to be aware of.

Inside these pages you will encounter:

❖ Profanity

❖ Kidnapping

❖ Violence

❖ Murder

❖ Emotional moments

❖ Rituals entwined with magic, prayer, and folklore

❖ Romance that ignites into explicit sensuality–Yes, there is sex

Disclaimer

In *Dangerous Desires,* my character Wahaya speaks a language that is based on the Cherokee language. Wahaya is a member of a tribe that no longer exists. Since I was unable to speak with any Cherokee officials to obtain more accurate spellings or phrasing of names and words, I did my best by combining various sources from Google and AI assistants.

The rituals and ceremonies in *Dangerous Desires* are my own creations and have not been taken from any official Native American tribes. Any mistakes or misrepresentations are entirely my own and were never meant to diminish, distort, or disrespect Cherokee or Native American heritage.

The names, words, and echoes of tradition within these pages are inspired by your culture, yet the folklore and mythology I have written come from my own imagination. They are not drawn from your sacred stories, but from the shadows of my creativity.

I have the utmost respect for Native Americans and their heritage. This book was created with sincere respect and admiration for all Native American people—past, present, and future

Table of Contents

Pronunciation Guide: iv

Content Advisory v

Disclaimer vi

Author's Note..viii

Chapter 1 1

Chapter 2 16

Chapter 3 29

Chapter 4 49

Chapter 5 59

Chapter 6 77

Chapter 7 90

Chapter 8 104

Chapter 9 113

Chapter 10 121

Chapter 11 130

Chapter 12 141

Chapter 13 152

Chapter 14 160

Chapter 15 169

Epilogue 173

Acknowledgments...177

About the Author 178

Author's Note

Thank you for taking the time to join the family and friends of *Dangerous Desires*. I recently became a fan of several YouTube channels that discuss Dogmen, and I've developed a curious fascination with these paranormal creatures.

I decided to explore them through folklore and romance, rather than portraying them as purely dangerous or evil.

I hope you enjoy their journey.

Thank you again, and I look forward to our next adventure together—whether it's *A Dating Die-Saster or Fun with My Scottish Brownie.*

Wishing you hugs, love, laughter, and many blessings!

Chapter 1

Oh my God, Ash! Wait, you caught him where? With… did you say your neighbor? I didn't think old Mrs. Simpson would be up to bedroom antics, isn't she like 90?" My best friend, Shana, said in a semi-serious tone.

I laughed so hard I thought my sides were going to split. I answered, "No, not Mrs. Simpson, silly, the other neighbor. Jessica Twilley—the short blonde with the enlarged upper area?" I answered, while gesturing 'big boobs' across my chest. "The worst part is, after I fed the cat, I heard a noise, so I went to check it out, and there they were going at it like rabbits. " I shivered and made a face, but kept going, "At least Jessica's cat got fed before I found them. Anyway, they saw me, I ran out of her place and into ours, slamming the door, locking Richard out. Within five minutes, he was banging on the door, yelling, 'It's not what you think, come on, Ash, open the door, can't we talk? She meant nothing, I swear, I care about you.'"

I tuned him out and began packing my stuff in every suitcase and box I could find. I had more boxes delivered from a moving company, which, surprisingly, arrived within the hour. So I packed everything that was mine. Fortunately, I didn't have that much that I wanted to keep, and I already had some things in storage. Richard wanted his things out; my stuff was too girly. So it paid off that I already had the storage. I was able to get Mrs. Simpson's son Jeff, you know the one who's had a bit of a crush on me for about a year now, to take everything—except what I brought with me to my storage unit. Then by the time I was done, I canceled my appointment and met with the landlord. Since my lease was about up, I let him know I was not renewing. And that Richard might be interested in the apartment, but that my name better not be anywhere on the lease. I may have implied legal action against both of them if it did. After that, since all my stuff and I were out of the apartment, I turned in my keys and came straight here. Oh, and I found out they had often done it in our apartment, while I was out. The landlord noticed."

Still trying to absorb what she heard, Shana asked, "Umm, what time of day did you say you found them? It sounds like this was early this morning, was it?

I tried to suppress a laugh, but a snicker escaped, "It was really early. I thought she was out of town, and since I had a 7:30 a.m. appointment, I decided to feed Mr. Fiestybutt around five, so they had probably been at it all night. Anyway... you know I've needed to visit my aunt for a long time. So, I figured it was time I took her up on her invitation, and before you ask, yes, she knows I'm stopping by here first. Oh, she did say to tell you that you guys are invited for the weekend, and we could have a celebration party of sorts."

After pausing for a second, Shana said, "Wow, Ash, you know Mark and I love you, but we could never figure out what you saw in Richard. Maybe his looks or his big *you know what,* but you've never been one for looks only. He didn't have brains, a sense of humor, and he never treated you with respect. I *never... ever...* liked Richard. I am sorry that the break-up happened the way it did, but I am soooo glad it's finally over. I get so angry thinking about how he whined like a baby to keep you from visiting your aunt or us. He didn't even do things to make you happy. So much stuff that you loved doing, he thought it was a waste of time, and when he told you that your photographs and drawings were crap, *while at one of your shows.* I could have killed him right then and there with my bare hands! You're too smart and gorgeous for that douche bag. You deserve, and can do, so much better. I was actually upset with you for believing his bullshit. Then, of course, Mark talked me down. We had to be patient and *pray* you came to your senses or caught him doing something—or someone."

Thinking about how I worried them saddened me; I didn't know how much it affected them, too. I looked at her with love for my friend and said, "Thank you for caring about me even when I was, apparently, oblivious. I get upset with myself, too, for allowing him to have had so much control over my life. I'm not sure what I was thinking or why I allowed myself to get so wrapped up in him. I mean, the sex was only good for about six months, and no matter the size, things still went downhill. But to stay with him for almost three years—I don't know what I was thinking. Maybe we were together just so we weren't alone, you know? He wasn't a bad guy; he just wasn't good for me. Who knows, maybe he and Jessica are perfect for each other."

"Well, are you going to at least stay the night and then head up the mountain tomorrow? We could drive up with you then." Shana's hands were propped up as if she were praying for me to say yes.

"Not tonight, but I do plan on coming back down once I get settled at Aunt Ulla's. I'm excited to see what she's done with the place. She also said she has a surprise for me—you know how much I love surprises. Plus, if you guys come up this weekend, we'll be able to visit more then."

Pouting, Shana agreed with a lop-sided smile, "Fine... I do know how you love surprises, well good ones anyway," she said, chuckling. "All right, don't stay the night. We'll just have a girls' night of wine, baking, and movies next time. Maybe at your aunt's! And now that you don't have to report to Richard, we'll have plenty of time to catch up." Glancing at the clock, she added, Mark should be home soon. Can you stay long enough to say hi? He would hate to miss you."

I thought for a moment before saying, "No, I have to get up the mountain before it gets too late. I have an idea for a new photo series, so I want to try to get some twilight shots over the valley. Heading up now should get me there at a perfect time to get some great shots—and you know me when I have a vision. I want to see it come to life as soon as possible."

Still talking as I headed into the kitchen to put my coffee cup in the sink, Shana met me at the opening of the room, and we both walked to the front door.

I promise I'll come back soon. Plus, if you come up this weekend, it'll be a little extra fun. Then one weekend when Mark is out hunting, I'll come stay with you, and we can go pamper ourselves with facials, massages, and movies. Now, I'd better get going before it's too dark and I'm too scared to stop. You know, bogeymen come out at dark." Giving her a hug goodbye, I had a strange feeling as I pulled out of the driveway.

An hour later, I stepped out of my car and almost immediately started taking shots of one of the most beautiful, picturesque scenes. It was early dusk, which added a special effect of light to the oncoming night sky. I was glad I took this route—it was absolutely one of the most beautiful places I'd been blessed to see in a long while. The sounds of nature and the sunset were soothing, which, apparently, I needed. The crickets were chirping, nightbirds were cooing, and along with an owl giving an occasional hoot—I couldn't have asked for a more serene moment. I stopped and took a few deep breaths to soak in the calm before getting a few last shots.

After my moment of Zen, I checked to make sure the shots I took with my camera and phone were good, then decided to head on up to my aunts. Tomorrow would be perfect to come back to this spot for more photos. It had such a dynamic view.

This location is definitely the spot to start the new series.

After memorizing a few landmarks so I'd be able to find the exact location again, I headed back across the road to my car. As I walked, I noticed all the birds cooing, and the crickets that were chirping had stopped. There was no noise, which was eerie, and something in me told me to move faster, but not to run. Suddenly, I heard something that was almost like a scream mixed with a growl coming from the woods. At that point, my feet had a mind of their own and increased my speed a bit.

All of a sudden, about twenty-ish yards up the road, a deer came bursting out of the trees, followed by a massive dog-like creature.

The photographer in me started recording video with my phone, while the scared part of me made sure my feet were moving faster—though I tried not to run. Even I knew you don't make noise or run from a predator who's that close. Thankfully, I hadn't locked my car when I got out, and with the creature occupied with the deer it had sadly caught and killed, I jumped in quickly. Honestly, the deer didn't have a chance of getting away from that thing.

As I closed my door, the creature stopped what it was doing, stood up straight, and slowly turned to face me. I was still recording with my phone as I started my car and rolled up the windows. How I kept recording is beyond me, but I did, and I watched half through my phone screen and half straight on, switching back and forth to make sure I kept the creature in frame—mainly because I was shaking. In the brief second it took me to glance at the screen, the creature had taken a few steps toward me, snarling, and looking like it thought it had just found its dessert.

Strangely, I could both hear and feel the deep resonating growl coming from this enormous creature. The vibrations went down my spine and then stirred somewhere I did not expect. The creature's ears were pulled back, making it look even more menacing. Then it stopped and sniffed the air, as if it had picked up the scent of new prey—which was probably me. Because it took one slow, calculated step toward me, growling again—except this time, it was...

What... wait...no... its ears were no longer pulled back, and I'll be... crap... it's smiling.

Seeing the creature's expression sent my brain into a twisted carnival of thoughts. Strange where the mind can take you during a stressful time.

Smiling, huh, wow... look at those teeth, bright and shiny pearly whites. Keep them far away from me.

As I looked closer, I was torn between being scared and strangely impressed. The creature was standing on two legs— its chest looked like it was chiseled, with hard muscles, as were its arms and legs. Its hands, not paws, but hands, were humanlike except it had long claws instead of fingernails.

My God, the creature was strikingly beautiful.

Its hair was coal black and silky looking. I had a strange desire to touch it, luckily, I knew better than to touch a wild wolf, let alone this thing. It was truly built like a human bodybuilder with a lot of hair, a long snout, and as I glanced from its head to toes...

Hmm, apparently it was all male.

The creature sniffed the air again, and this time it was definitely smiling. I heard a deep, gravelly voice in my head say, "Like me, do you?" He lifted his head and took in an even deeper breath.

Well, crap—it talks! What the hell?!

Its voice was deep, dark, and scarily sexy.

What is wrong with me? I've been reading too many werewolf books lately. I can't believe my body is having a reaction to this creature. No more werewolf books. Oh, shit, shit, shit, he just took a step closer, what am I doing? I need to get out of here.

The creature is... Oh my God... is it laughing at me? Now I feel insulted.

I put my car in reverse, floored it, and paused only long enough to make a U-turn, then sped away. As I flew down the road, I heard his voice in my head, "You can't run from me, I have your scent, human. I will find you."

For some silly reason, I answered the voice, "Why would you want to find me? I didn't do anything to you or your meal! Plus, I doubt I'd taste good, and I'm probably not your type, so go back to your dinner and forget you ever saw me."

To my surprise, the voice answered back, "Won't forget... You... are... mine."

With that, I sped away, hearing deep, throaty laughter in my head.

I screamed out loud to myself, "What the hell was that?! A werewolf, Anubis, a figment of my imagination, what? And now it's going to come after me. Why? "You are mine." What the hell does that mean?! No one's going to believe me. God, I hope I got pictures to prove what I saw."

Flying down the mountain road, swerving and all, was not the brightest idea, but I was not about to slow down... not yet. Once I felt like I was far enough away, I began to calm down and go the speed limit. By the time I made it back to the main road, I had almost convinced myself the creature didn't exist. Surely—I was just tired and a little more upset than I thought over everything that had happened with Richard.

I headed back to Shana and Mark's. It wasn't too late, and I'm pretty sure they'll be okay with me heading back. She wanted me to stay the night, well, after what just happened to me, now I will.

As I pulled into the driveway, I was relieved to see both their cars and the living room lights on. I bet they'd find this interesting—since both of them are interested in supernatural stuff.

Shana has been a nurse practitioner for over 15 years and has seen some strange things during her hospital rotation. Mark, her husband, was the local sheriff, an avid hunter, and, strangely enough, also interested in the supernatural. Apparently, he and one of his deputies had a brief encounter with something that put him on a research journey to educate himself and his department, just in case there was another run-in. Maybe they knew of some new hybrid wolf that'd been released in the woods and could help assure me that I wasn't going crazy.

As I got out of my car, I had a strange, almost creepy, feeling that I was being watched. I started to argue with myself about calling Shana before barging in, but before I knew it, my flight response took over, and I was banging on their door and yelling, "Shana, Mark! Hello? Are you guys up?!"

The feeling of being watched was growing stronger, and my knocking grew more hectic.

Damn, did the thing follow me?

Mark threw open the door and was about to yell when he realized it was me, then he noticed the look on my face. "Ash! What the... are you okay?" He asked as he stepped outside and began looking around, sensing my fear.

"Ash, you look like you've seen a ghost!" Shana said, coming into the living room. "Oh my God, girl, what is wrong? Sit down and tell us, I'll get you some water—or do you want something stronger?"

Feeling a little silly, I muttered, "Stronger, please."

With a drink in hand and the two of them now sitting, they stared at me, waiting for me to say something. I downed the Scotch Shana brought me, still not sure where to start.

I cleared my throat, "Hmm, you know how I was heading up to Aunt Ursula's?"

They looked at me and nodded their heads in unison, then Shana added, "I thought you would have been there by now."

"Yeah, well, I was on my way but decided to stop and get some good shots from the old road route. The sun was setting, and the valley below, with the surrounding mountain view. It was beautiful, and I got caught up in the view...."

Apparently, I was taking way too long to get to the point, so Mark leaned forward and asked, "And did something happen...?"

Hesitantly, I said, "Ah, yes, I was almost back to my car when a deer charged frantically out of the woods with something chasing it..."

Mark leaned in even closer, now wide-eyed, like a kid at Christmas looking at all the lights, toys, and goodies, and asked, "What was it? How large? Please tell me you got a picture of whatever it was."

Shana smacked him, "Shhh, let her talk. You can play twenty questions later."

With a slight grimace, I carried on, "I'm not sure what it was, but it was huge—crazy huge—beautiful, wolf-like creature."

Mark couldn't hold back, "You saw the dogman? Now I really hope you got pictures."

I stood up and wrung my hands, "I guess so. I mean, I thought of a werewolf when I saw it, but there was something different from what I read about werewolves. So... I guess it was—what did you call it? A dogman?" I shrugged with uncertainty.

Shana, the calmest one of us, said, "Mark, be quiet and let her finish. Ash, please continue and disregard the child who is my husband."

At that, we laughed—at least Shana and I did. Mark, on the other hand, looked a little pouty.

"Okay, well," I continued, "I got in my car, and I guess it heard when I shut the door... but... did you know they can talk? Well, kind of. And it smiled, scary as it sounds, it smiled at me."

Mark looked so excited, he was about to jump out of his chair, and asked, "It talked to you, what did it say? What did it do—"

Before he could finish, Shana clamped her hand over his mouth. "Sweetheart, let... her... finish!"

I started pacing again, then looked at both of them sitting in front of me. I heard my words play back in my head and started to laugh, "Umm, the creature caught the deer and killed it, so I slipped back to my car. It was like, I don't know, 20 to 25 yards away, I guess, but when I closed the door... well, it stopped what it was doing, stood up—on two legs, with its ears back—and it sniffed the air as it slowly turned around to look at me. Of course, I was also trying to record at the same time, which I don't think he liked, because he growled. His growl was a deep, vibrating, scary growl. Then, I swear it smiled. It moved closer, sniffed the air again, a long, deep sniff, and this time it definitely smiled right at me. I'm pretty sure he was enjoying my reaction to him. Which was, and still is, embarrassing—I'll explain later."

Mark, who was now biting his lip and, literally, sitting on the edge of his seat, quietly asked, "What... did... it... say...?"

"Oh, that. Umm, it was rather cocky when it talked. If I can remember correctly, I believe it said something like... 'I smell your desire. You can't run from me. I have your scent, human. I will find you.' Oh, and when I told it to forget it saw me, it said, 'Won't forget, you are mine.' Other than laughing at me, that was about it."

Trying to rush past the desire I had mentioned, I hurried to ask what they thought. "So, what do you think he meant by all that?"

Then I had an 'a-ha' moment, and I panicked, "Oh my God! What if it followed me here? I was driving as fast as I could, but when I got here and stepped out of the car, I felt like I was being watched. Surely you don't think it did... please no... it couldn't have, right? Surely, not with how fast I was going... I had to be going at least 80, 90, maybe even more after I reached the main road. I'd hate to bring it here to your house. God, that would be horrible."

At that point, I took a deep breath to steady myself, panic setting in at the thought that I might have led that creature straight to my best friend's house.

Shana and Mark exchanged a look with each other, then Shana spoke first, "Well, if it is a *he* like you seem to think, and it is what Mark *hopes* it is," Shana gave Mark a side eye, but continued. "Umm, maybe he, umm, how do I say this without sounding like a romance writer…"

Before she could tactfully formulate the words, Mark blurted out, "He's going to claim you as his mate, is what it could mean."

I looked at both of them and frantically shook my head, "NO! That's not possible… is it? I mean, he's all furry like a wolf, and yes, it was all male, I could tell, especially as he took a few steps towards me. Even though it stood upright like a person and was, well, built like a huge ass bodybuilder—he had fur and a head sort of like a wolf. So, it's not possible, right? You two are joking—maybe we've all read one too many werewolf romance books?"

Shana could hear the panic rising in my tone, so in an attempt to calm me down, she said, "Well, for example, it could be more like where animals have formed attachments or bonds with humans, some almost instantly—it could be like that. Let's not worry about that right now. You need to calm down and get some rest. Then in the morning we can figure something out, okay?"

As Shana was calming me, Mark walked over to his desk and sat at his computer. As he was typing, he was mumbling mostly to himself, but still loud enough that we could hear him. "But if it is a hybrid of sorts, it might think of her more as a mate. Could be that if her body reacted strongly enough to the vibration of its growl and her body had put off a scent, he was attracted..."

Shana glanced over to Mark, then back to me, and realized I could hear what Mark was saying. So, she quickly barked for him to keep his thoughts to himself.

But it was too late. My anxiety was spiking just thinking about the situation all over again, so I looked over to Shana, pleading, "What am I going to do? When he, it, whatever, spoke to me, it was in my head. And when I was talking to myself, it understood and heard me, or my thoughts, I don't know which, but it heard me. When I got out of my car, here, I felt like I was being watched—hence the frantic banging. What do you think it's going to do? I'm just getting my life together with this move. I've never been this scared, not even when I was locked in that scary funeral home after hours."

This time, Mark spoke up, "As you should be, scared, I mean. The tales I've heard are scary. Although if it's a dogman, I don't recall hearing of them ever killing anyone. Scaring the crap out of people, and mostly killing animals. Possibly hurting humans but not killing them. At least the stories I've read. Who knows, maybe it just wanted to scare you away from the deer. You did interrupt its dinner."

"Ew, poor deer. It succeeded—so much so, I'm definitely not going to my aunt's tonight, or maybe ever again, if that's the only road up the mountain. I wonder if she has ever had any run-ins with it. Anyway, is the invitation to stay still open? I... I don't want to leave the house, especially in the dark."

"Of course, hon, you know you can stay. And tomorrow the three of us can do some research or drive up to your aunt's house. I'll ride with you, and Mark can follow us in his car.

Just know, if you don't feel safe, you can come back here, and we'll figure something out from there, okay?"

I sighed. "Okay, but I'm thinking I might not stay with her now. I might look into a few Airbnbs, hotels, maybe another town, possibly a different country. I don't want to drive up there again... maybe ever. But I can't leave my aunt stranded knowing it's roaming around. I'm not sure what to do. I'll call her in the morning. But for now, I'll just text her before I go to sleep and say that I lost track of time and won't be able to make it tonight. So she doesn't worry. Hmm... I wonder if I could get her to move?"

Shana sighed as she pulled me in for a hug with a slight chuckle and said, "You're just scared right now. You know your aunt would never leave that place—dog, wolf, man, or whatever. Hell, she'd make it move first. She can be scary, too, you know. Sleep on it tonight, and then tomorrow morning we can figure out what to do, okay? Come with me, and I'll get you settled upstairs. Since you were last here, we've turned Jamie's old room into a guest room after she moved to England, and Tyler won't be home from camp for another three weeks. Oh, do you want anything from your car? Mark can grab your luggage."

Without hesitation, I blurted, "NO, no, no, thank you, but no! No one needs to go outside. I'll be okay until morning, I think." And gave her a half-smile, half-grimace.

Shana laughed as she guided me upstairs to the hall closet, where she grabbed me a toothbrush, extra blanket, pillow, towels, and one of her sleeping shirts.

"Don't worry. We'll figure this out, okay? Just get some sleep—or at least try to." She reassured me again.

I hugged and thanked her before going into the guest room. I heard Mark come up the steps, and he said goodnight through the door. Then his and Shana's bedroom door closed for the night.

While getting ready for bed, I replayed the day's events over and over in my mind. I stepped out into the hallway and quickly darted into the bathroom. I brushed my teeth, freshened up a bit, then quietly slipped back into the guest room. As I changed into the sleep shirt, I noticed the house seemed overly quiet—which is strange—but then again, I'm also used to a busy, noisy city, not the outskirts where there are no sirens, loud people next door, or just noise. I was beyond ready to lie down now and try to forget as much as possible. The moment my head touched the pillow, I was out.

Chapter 2

It was strange for me to fall asleep so fast, especially after the events of the day. But my exhaustion pulled me deep into a dream world that I was unfamiliar with...

~

I found myself standing in what appeared to be a clearing in the woods. A huge blood red moon hung eerily brightly in a dark sapphire sky. Haunting but beautiful all the same. It kind of reminded me of a jeweler's cloth where they pour out diamonds to show their vibrancy. There weren't very many diamonds scattered across the sky, though, and the moon burned like an inferno, fiery blood light spilling from its edges. It was so big and bright I didn't feel illuminated — I felt marked, as if the darkness itself had chosen me. Standing in the void, I couldn't hear much, but I somehow knew I was not alone.

Deep in my bones, I felt it was the creature, hiding in the shadows as he watched me. Noticing a heaviness to the darkness, I knew it was him. He was the predator—I was the prey. I felt his stare along my spine, so I turned to look in his direction. He released a low, guttural growl that vibrated me to my core, and then he opened his eyes. Brilliant, scarlet eyes pierced through the darkness to find their target. Me. I felt heat travel through my body, igniting a fire that seemed to give me courage. I yelled, "Come out and face me, stop hiding like a coward!"

He slowly stepped out of the shadows, an evil smile crept across his lips as he stalked toward me, each step vibrated through the ground and ran up my spine as he came closer. He glared at me the whole way, devouring me with his eyes. I hadn't realized how big he was until he was standing in front of me. I found my gaze traveling up from his massive, clawed feet to his muscled legs. I hurried upward, quickly skipping over the undeniable proof of his size, and made my way to his sculpted abs—pure muscles. I had a desire to reach up and touch him, to see if his fur was as soft as it looked or coarse. I could feel the heat of his stare on me. Then I looked up into his eyes—his stare had softened, as had his smile. Never taking his eyes away from mine, he lifted a claw and tenderly ran it down my cheek. He began to slowly circle me, touching me almost sensually. He leaned in and breathed in my scent as his claw tenderly raked over me.

In my mind, I heard, "Your scent is known to my spirit. You are mine." As he came back in front of me, he leaned down, now eye to eye, he closed his eyes and drew in one last deep breath, only to vanish in a black fog.

~

Next thing I knew, I was awakened by Shana knocking on the door, "Ash, are you awake? Hello ...Ash... Wakey, wakey! Ashley... wake up!"

Still half asleep, I answered, "I'm almost awake."

Shana stopped knocking, "Well, I'm heading down to make breakfast, and I can have coffee waiting for you if you're ready. Do you need anything?"

Still tired and now confused, I didn't want to wake up, but I knew that I must, so I yelled back to the door, "I'm awake, I'll be down shortly. And, yes please, a huge cup of coffee."

Feeling foggy from the dream as I sat up, I ran over to the door to crack it and yelled, "Shana, I hate to ask, but could Mark get my small suitcase for me, please? It's in the passenger seat with my camera bag, and I think my keys are on the coffee table."

As if we were still in our college days, Shana yelled back, "On it," then proceeded to yell to Mark, "Please get Ash's small suitcase out of the car; her keys are probably on the table."

Mark, now in on the shouting fun, "Don't you want both of them? I mean, you ladies need choices, right?"

Now I opened the door all the way, Shana and I both still laughing, and yelled, "Just the small one, please."

Next thing we heard was the front door closing as Mark went running out to grab the suitcase. In the meantime, I put on the robe Shana handed me, and we went downstairs for some coffee. Within a few minutes, the front door opened, and Mark looked like he'd seen a ghost but was happy about it.

He looked at both of us and slowly said, "You two need to see Ash's car. I think she has an admirer."

Shana looked at me, shrugged, then all three of us headed out the front door to see what had Mark acting so strange. As we walked around the back of the car where Mark was indicating, there was the dead deer from last night, and something carved into my car's bumper.

"Holy shit," was all I could get out. They looked at me, and Shana grabbed my hand.

"Ash, I'm so glad you didn't go back outside last night, you might have run into your dogman, or someone playing a sick joke!"

As I backed away from the scene a few steps, it looked like the scratches might've spelled something...

"Does that say... mine?" I looked at Shana, then Mark, now pissed and scared I gruffed out, "The fucker can spell? What am I dealing with here? It can't be a wild animal, can it?"

Shana moved to hug me while Mark interjected a little unwelcomed knowledge, "From what I've heard, they are extremely intelligent, and I'm not sure if it's a hybrid between dog and man, or alien, or demon. No one knows, but there are several folklores out there, some are Native American, some from the Appalachian area. Hell, some even mention creatures coming through portals. I can help you research more if you want, but I think you need to know more about what it is and what your options are."

Shana gave Mark a look that said for him to be quiet, then she chimed in, "I think we need to talk to your aunt first. With her living up on the mountain as long as she has, she may know something or at least have heard of the thing. We *have* to go see her. I'll ride with you, and Mark can follow us."

I knew she saw the fear on my face as I began to speak, "I don't think I want to stay in the area. Europe is sounding rather nice right now."

Mark stepped in, continuing, "Ash, I don't think you can escape it just by going to Europe. It's going to take more than relocation to another country. It may have, kind of, marked you? And I hate to scare you, but I seriously think it would follow or find you even if you moved to another country. It might take a while, but I think it would. We're going to have to look at ways to get rid of it or at least understand what's going on so we can deal with it."

"Crap, did I do something to deserve this?" I asked no one in particular, "I don't need this. I just want to work, hide away for a while, and enjoy time with my aunt and you guys." Tears slipped out before I could catch them—not in sobs, but enough to quicken my breath and make my head spin. I didn't understand why it hit so hard.

Shana hurriedly tried to calm me, "Mark, I think she's going into shock, help me get her into the house. Maybe grab some smelling salts and a paper bag too, just in case."

Mark and Shana guided me back into the house and sat me on the couch. Mark ran to the kitchen to get some water while Shana sat holding my hand and soothingly rubbing my back.

I took a few deep breaths to try and calm myself, I let them know that I was okay but still spooked. Mark looked me over, then spoke to Shana in a bit of a hushed tone, "We need to find out what's going on and make sure she's safe. I'm going to call one of my deputies to come get the deer while I go see if I can clean up her car and possibly smooth out the scratches." He then looked back at me, patted me on the shoulder, and went back outside.

Feeling anxious, I blurted out, "Shana- I can't—I don't think I can drive up there, not now."

Letting out a big sigh, she handed me my coffee and said, "How about I drive your car, we will talk to your aunt, and maybe find out a few things. You can also stay here tonight if you want. I won't let you out of my sight, I promise. Plus, Mark probably won't either, okay? Does that sound like a plan?"

Trying to lighten the mood a little, I half-joked, "You can keep an eye on me, but not Mark. He'll drive me crazy with repeated questions. But yes, I guess that's doable, especially since I don't want to impose on you two. I really do need to figure out where I'm going to live. All my stuff is in storage for another two months. After that, I need to have a place to put everything. I was supposed to move in with Aunt Ulla, but I don't know if I can with this dog-thing after me."

Shana agreed with a nod and a sip of her coffee, then continued with her plan, "I completely understand, but like I said, let's go to your aunt's, see what info she might have, then take steps from there. I seriously don't think this creature wants to hurt you—it's possibly more drawn to you than anything. We'll research and talk about options from there. Who knows, maybe it was a one-time thing, and he just wanted to scare you. You did interrupt his meal."

I thought back to my dream, "Ahhh... I need to tell you something. I had a strange dream after I fell asleep. The creature was there, at first hidden in the shadows. When he came forward, he had a wicked smile, and he said *I smelled like mine*—well, his, you know what I mean. Then you were knocking on the door and, *poof*, he was gone in a puff of black fog. I didn't want to wake up, but you did mention coffee, and I couldn't resist. Coffee or creature... coffee won," I added with a quick laugh.

At that moment, Mark walked in and said he had gotten my car cleaned up, but the scratches were too deep, so he wasn't able to get them completely out.

"So, when are we heading up the mountain? My deputy just picked up the deer and let me know there's a pretty big snowstorm headed this way, expected to hit late tonight or early tomorrow. I think we need to get going. And we might also want to be prepared with extra clothes just in case we get stuck up there for a few days." Then he ran upstairs, I assume, to get some bags packed for him and Shana.

Shana looked at me for a reaction, "We can wait till after the storm if you'd prefer, since it sounds like it's going to be a big storm, but either way we need to call your aunt and let her know something."

I nodded my head then, picked up my phone, and called my aunt. She must have been sitting nearby because she answered before the first ring ended.

"Ash, are you okay? After your text last night and the strange feeling I had this morning, I was worried something might have happened to you. Are you still coming today?"

Doing my best not to sound nervous or upset, I took a steadying breath before I answered, "I'm fine, Aunt Ulla. We're trying to decide when to leave because there's a snowstorm on the way. Do you need supplies? If you need them, we can get them, and then we'll head up. Shana will be driving with me, and Mark will follow us. They can be prepared to stay the night. So, how are you on supplies for a storm?"

Aunt Ulla realized I was rambling, "Ash, dear! Slow down. I have enough to weather this storm for us all and, as much as I want to see you, it's your choice if you come before or after."

Now it was my turn for a weird feeling. Aunt Ulla's tone was different, and the fact that she was giving me a choice with no suggestions on making said choice felt off. I know it's been a while since we'd last talked, but I felt she wasn't telling me something. I made the quick decision that we were going. I wasn't going to leave her up there alone during a storm, even though she'd done it for years. Something felt different, and I became protective, especially with the creature around the mountain. We were going regardless of my previous fears.

"Aunt Ulla, we're coming, we'll be leaving here as soon as Shana and Mark get some stuff together and I change clothes. Are you sure there isn't anything you need or want us to bring?"

Sounding a bit strange, Aunt Ulla went quiet for a moment and then asked to talk to Mark for a minute. I went upstairs and gave Mark the phone. I busied myself, getting ready and making sure I had everything repacked. He talked to her for over ten minutes, with his side sounding like a polite schoolboy, "*Yes, ma'am, no ma'am, yes, ma'am, yes ma'am I will, I know who that is, yes, I can do that, thank you ma'am, okay thank you, I'm on it, and then here's Ash again, see you soon.*"

I took the phone and gave him a *what the hell, Mr. Scared-of-my-aunt* look, "Hello again, what do you want us to bring?"

She sounded better, but her tone was still a bit strange, "Mark knows what to pick up, so don't worry. Unless you're craving something particular like cardboard pizza, chips, or candy, no. I remember your salty-sweet tooth, but you don't need to worry about picking up any food. Mark will pick up the extra supplies. Alright, dear, I'll see the three of you soon. Be careful on the drive and don't stop on the way up, okay? I'm going to start getting things ready. Be safe, and I can't wait to see you. Love you, and I'll see you soon, bye dear."

Before I could say anything else, the phone went silent. She hung up. I guess she had more to get ready since there were three of us coming.

My Aunt Ursula, or Aunt Ulla, as my friends and I like to call her, is usually... talkative. She's a selective socializer and chooses interactions on her terms, which are very few and far between. But when she does, she is a blast to be around.

Maybe she's just concerned we might get stuck in the storm?

I took my stuff downstairs to see Shana setting her suitcase at the front door.

"Hey Shana, did my aunt seem okay the last time you were up there? Because I think she was acting a little strange on the phone. Do you know if anything's bothering her?

"Ash, you know your aunt, we'll find out when she wants us to know. Plus, you might be projecting. After all, you did just have a horrifying experience," she said as she collected our cups, straightening things as she went.

"She didn't say anything while you guys were up there, did she?"

Stopping to think for a second, Shana turned, "She did mention that she had help with some of the renovations, but we didn't see anyone. Oh, and she did have a date around the same time. Not sure how it went though, I talked to her or been back up since then."

A bit surprised, I asked, "She's dating, and you didn't think to mention it? She didn't tell me that either, or that she had major renovations done. Why didn't she tell me? Wow, I need to make sure she's not gotten herself in over her head."

Shana started laughing, "Look who's being all adult and protective. It's cute, but I think she can take care of herself."

"Well, yes, she may have raised me, but I have to make sure she's not getting into something crazy or weird. There are way too many scammers who could take advantage of her, or a Casanova who breaks her heart. Someone has to watch out for her."

Now both of us were laughing. Shana and I walked outside, where Mark was waiting for us.

I figured Mark could use a little extra space, so I asked, "Mark, why not put your bags in my car too, since you're picking up supplies for my aunt and may need the extra room?"

He quickly agreed and put his bag in my trunk.

I opened the door to my car, but before I jumped in, I turned to the couple giving each other a quick hug and kiss goodbye, "Hey guys, thank you for helping me, listening to the craziness I experienced with little to no judgement, and well, for being my sane friends. It's not every day your bestie tells you she's had a run-in with a dogman and you react calmly, so thank you."

Shana and Mark then came over and hugged me, and Shana said, "That's what friends are for. Plus, I live vicariously through you. But Ash, no more Richards, I'd rather you date the dogman than Richard."

We all laughed, and then Mark had to be the sensible one, "Now that we've decided who Ash can or cannot date next, let's get going. Luggage is in the car, and I have errands to run, so let's go, ladies."

Shana and I headed back into the house for one last potty break before the long drive, while Mark left. Apparently, he had several stops to make for my aunt. He wouldn't tell us what she asked for, just that he had to make a few stops before meeting us up there. We also gave him our list of snacks we wanted from the store. Shana said we should only be ahead of him by about 30 minutes unless he gets carried away and goes on a shopping spree, or stops to gossip, then it could be hours. We giggled at the mention of men gossiping while Shana added a few extra things to the car that I hadn't thought to bring for snowy mountain weather driving, like an emergency kit, blankets, water, and even more snacks for the drive. You would think this was a cross-country trip instead of an hour and a half, maybe two hours away at the most.

I started the drive but when we stopped to fill up on gas, Shana took over since we were now near the base of the mountain. It wasn't that long of a drive, but I didn't want to be the one driving past the spot where I met the creature.

As we drove closer to the spot where I encountered the dogman, I surprised myself and asked Shana to pull off to the side of the road. She asked, "Are you sure? Because I think we should just keep driving, and your aunt said not to stop."

"I'm sure," I replied, "I need to see if there is any proof for myself that it was real. I glanced at the video briefly, then the photos from yesterday's dogman introduction, and they were all blurry. So, I need to see if there were any signs of the creature or deer, *something* left here in this spot to let me know I wasn't going crazy."

So, Shana pulled my car into the spot where I had parked before. The road on this mountain was narrow, barely enough for two cars—not much room for error with mountains.

I knew it was the same spot because there was only forest and uphill on that side of the road with the one small pull-off, and on the other side was nothing but a guardrail and downhill. I got out and walked around looking at the ground, but didn't see anything unusual. Nothing to show that anyone or anything had been here. I remember clearly that this was the spot. I was on the other side of the road, directly across from my car, when the deer ran out of the woods.

I wandered up towards where the dogman came out after the poor deer, nothing —no blood, hair, or footprints. Shana, still sitting in the car in case we needed to peel out quickly, yelled after me, "Are you sure about that? I wouldn't get too close in case he's still out here!"

"He came out of the woods this way!" I yelled back, "And, besides, you're yelling loud enough that any animal within eight miles would run the other direction."

I heard her laugh at that. I continued to look around until I was thoroughly confused. There was nothing. I was standing in the spot where I was sure the deer had died, and *nothing*. I knew I was in the right spot, except there was no physical evidence, but the heaviness in the air told me I was right. I made my way back to the car and hopped in.

"Anything?" Shana asked as I closed my door.

I looked back at where I was just standing and said, "Yes, there's the cluster of trees I was shooting—the one with wildflowers around the base."

From here, I could see my tire tracks from where I peeled out, and there was—

Wait... what the hell?

Shana put the car in drive and began moving forward, but I stopped her quickly, "Shana! Wait! Stop the car."

"What the —" but I was out of the car before she could finish. I ran over to the edge of the forest, a little farther up than I was a minute ago. A huge footprint was etched into the dirt. Standing over it, I realized *that* was the spot my car was in... Shana put the car in park and ran over to me, "Ash, what is it? Woah..."

We glanced at each other, and I took several photos of the print with my phone, then we hurried back to the car.

"Shana, let's get to my aunt's house quickly."

As we pulled out, I looked back at the tree line, and I could swear I saw a huge shadowy figure step out of the trees.

"Shana, floor it!"

And we sped out, heading to my aunt's. We still had around an hour left until we reached the lodge, so we sped up and locked the doors.

Once we were on the road for a few minutes, Shana glanced over, "You look a little peaked, did you see something back there?"

"Honestly, I thought I saw the shadow of him step out as we were pulling away, but I'm not sure. Didn't want to take any chances, though. Plus, Mark would kill me if something happened to you because we stopped there." I said while glancing back again.

"Oh, he'd be upset with both of us, not just you," Shana chuckled, and we slowly drifted into our own worlds.

Chapter 3

With the lull of the car in motion and the steady sound of the wheels on the road, I drifted into a haze of memories. The rhythm took me deeper with each mile.

At first, my thoughts were consumed by the fact that I hadn't spoken to my aunt in months. We used to talk several times a week, and I'd even gotten her to do FaceTime once. She'd ask when I was coming to visit, then Richard would interrupt us and need my attention, wanting me to cut the call short. Then things always seemed to come up for some reason or another, usually something Richard wanted. He didn't care for my aunt; maybe he could sense that she saw through his bullshit. I wasn't sure why I let him dictate when I could visit or talk to anyone, but sadly, I did.

Richard was a lead carpenter who looked really good in his tool belt and knew it. In retrospect, I should have known things wouldn't last; he was more into how he looked to others than to us as a couple. I caught him flirting several times, but he would always talk me out of being upset with him. He had a knack for bs-ing me into thinking he was just being nice, or trying to make contacts for new jobs, and that it was his nature to smile at everyone. I found out he was screwing several of his clients, a few of the secretaries at the company he worked through, and our next-door neighbor. Through our three years together, it finally came out that he was faithful for maybe the first six to eight months of it, and that was all. When I caught him at the neighbors', I was thankful that he had the decency to go to her place, at least that time anyway.

It was funny, I had caught him by accident too—he'd been really good at hiding things until Jessica, our neighbor, asked me to check on her cat when I could. He had been sick, and since I pretty much worked from home, I didn't mind. Her mistake though? She gave me a key and mixed up her weekends on when she would be going to a friend's place for two days or maybe she did it on purpose. Wanted me to find them—who knows.

I went in to feed Mr. Fluffybutt, the cat, only to find it was a different fluffy butt being fed... by Richard. I can't believe I locked him out of the apartment, packing everything so fast, and then moved my stuff—it was satisfying. When I talked to the landlord, he completely understood and confirmed what had been going on. He was okay with me breaking the lease a little early and didn't charge me any penalties. He said he would miss me as a tenant, and on a funny note, since Richard wasn't officially on the lease, he just might call the police on him or try to rent him the apartment at a bit higher amount. But he promised I wouldn't be listed anywhere on those papers. As soon as everything was taken care of, I called my aunt and let her know I was coming to visit. I asked if I could stay a little bit, and figured I would look for a place around her area later.

Then my thoughts drifted to the dream and the creature that had come out of the shadows and called me 'his.' Would there be a repeat of the dream tonight? Why do I want that answer to be yes? More importantly, why do I get heated when I think about the creature?

I don't have time for this crap!

I was so lost in my thoughts that I hadn't noticed we were now sitting in the lodge's driveway, and Shana was trying to get my attention.

"Ash, Ash... Hello, Earth to Ash... Are you okay? Dang girl, you were on another planet. So far away... Where were you?"

"Sorry, I was remembering why I'm moving in the first place and the dream. I'm good, though. Let's go in."

I opened my door, but Shana stopped me before I got out.

Shana reached over, putting her hand on my arm, and looked at me with concerned eyes, "I'm sorry you're going through this, but personally, I'm glad you got rid of him. You deserve better."

"Thank you, and I'm glad too. When I caught him cheating, I was just grateful he wasn't in our place, at least this time. I wasn't all that upset with what I had seen, honestly, I was relieved. I'd gotten comfortable with things even though I wasn't happy. It was time it ended. I only wish I hadn't seen them in all their bare-assed-glory. That was gross!"

I laughed as I climbed out of the car and met Shana at the trunk to grab our stuff.

"He wasn't looking that good in his carpenter belt anymore anyway."

Then both of us were laughing hard, and Shana added, "I bet your Aunt Ulla was thrilled when you told her. I don't think she really liked him; she has a sort of sixth sense, it's a little scary how accurate she can be. Hell, remember I made sure to get her approval on Mark before we got married? I was too head over heels to be sensible, and I brought him here. Right off the bat, they became best friends, she gave me a thumbs up, and we've been together ever since. She even told me if I didn't nab that man, she would."

We were both laughing even harder at this point. Shana handed me my keys, and we grabbed our bags, then walked up to the front door. On our walk up the stairs, I stopped for a second to smell the forest and breathe in nature.

I held my head up to the sky with my eyes closed, "God, I missed this place."

All of a sudden, I felt like I was being watched again. I looked over at Shana, and she was obviously feeling it too. At that moment, Aunt Ulla opened the door, greeting us, but quickly saw the looks on our faces. She came out, grabbed a couple of bags from us, and ushered us inside quickly.

Now that we were standing in the foyer, I looked around, realizing I had forgotten how huge this place was. No wonder she was going to rent out a few rooms. Although I wasn't sure anyone would want to stay if they knew what's out in the woods, it is a beautiful place for solitude, though.

Maybe a writer's retreat would be good here and, in the summer, an artist workshop.

This has some possibilities. I could help her with Marketing... grrr... I have to stop plus; I'm getting way ahead of myself. I don't even know if I'm going to stay. It's just that walking through the doors felt like being home again, which is a good thing, but I can't walk in and take over. Damn, I regret being away for so long.

My aunt noticed me looking around. She walked over smiling and gave me a big hug, "I'm so glad to have you home, Ash. It's been way... too... long."

I hugged her back and refocused on my aunt, "I know, I was just thinking about that. I'm so sorry I let Richard control my time and keep me away. I should have—" She stopped me with a shush.

"Water under the bridge, my dear. I am grateful you finally saw what we all tried to tell you. But you had to figure it out on your own, or else you might have resented us, and I didn't want that. So, let's get your stuff upstairs in your new apartment. That is, if you want it, I'm not going to force you to stay, but I would love to have you move in here." She let go of me, grabbed my luggage, and started up the stairs.

I followed after he, "Apartment? Umm…But, Aunt Ulla, I would need at least three rooms, and I can't take that space from you. Don't you need to rent those rooms."

She half shrugs, "Nonsense, my dear, there are enough rooms between the main floor and the cabins I had built for me to rent, and I'm having the old barn remodeled into a meeting and events space. I built a new barn to house all the animals." She glanced back at me for a moment, "So, I could use your help, and I hope you don't get upset with me… but I have already remodeled four of the upstairs rooms for you. Though if you don't want to stay here, I won't be upset. I will still want your opinion and help with marketing, but I won't be upset…"

Once we reached the top landing, she handed me three keys. Then she gestured to half of the doors at the landing and said, "This portion of the top floor is yours. The door on the left is your office, the door on the right is your studio and darkroom, and the middle two open into your living area. I combined two rooms into one; that's why there are two doors. The one key opens both. Now, I know you have some furniture of your own, but I put some stuff in until you decide what you want to do. You can keep all of this if you want—in fact, a few pieces belonged to your mom, so they're yours anyway."

I unlocked the office door first, and it took my breath away. I knew my aunt was a sweetheart, but she thought of everything. Knowing how I loved the colors in nature, she combined a few to make up my office. As I stepped into the room, I noticed buttercream-yellow curtains against the walls that were painted a pale sage green. Surprisingly, she even painted the ceiling a light blue, giving it an open sky feel.

A weathered oak desk was set partially under the window so that you could look outside, yet were still able to see the office door. On the desk sat a rose quartz pen holder next to a stack of notebooks with indigo, plum, and rust-colored covers. Above the desk, she hung a corkboard framed in antique bronze, with some of my favorite quotes and affirmations pinned to it, feather-shaped paper clips, and my uncle's old brass compass.

When I was little, he once said he would always find his way home as long as he had his compass. I guess she's letting me know I've found my way home. Smiling to myself, I looked up to see string lights with a warm, white hue woven along the wall, intertwined with a vine of faux ivy and a few clipped photos of castles, oceans, and forests. Photos I took.

Over in the other corner, near the balcony door, was my mother's large, round, velvety, charcoal gray reading chair. It looked rather plush and inviting with two throw pillows—one in deep cranberry red that was embroidered with the words, 'Choose a path, they all lead somewhere,' and the other in royal blue that said, 'It's what you believe that makes something good or bad.'

Mom loved those quotes; she and her best friend lived by them. I picked one up and smelled it, an old habit I started after she died, trying to find remnants of her in any way I could. Unfortunately, nothing left. I sighed and lay the pillow back down and glanced around the room again. I noticed one of the walls had a beautiful bookshelf that was stained with a rich, espresso brown. I walked over to look at the few books my aunt had placed there, a few of my uncle's, a few of my mom's, and a few of hers. I ran my hand across the spines as tears began to prick my eyes again.

I heard my aunt clear her throat and say, "I thought you might like to add those to your collection. Now all it needs are… yours."

I rushed over and gave my aunt one of the biggest hugs, "I love you. This is better than anything I could have designed for myself. You thought of everything, including me. Thank you, I love it. Now I want to see the studio. If it's anything like what you did in here…" I trailed off as I gave her an extra hug and ran to open the studio door.

I gasped as the door swung open—this was the setup I had often envisioned. A small studio space next to my living quarters and office. Immediately to the right of the door were spots to hang finished photos and a rack for drying prints. There was a darkroom tucked into one corner, with just enough room to process film and surrounded by a floor-length blackout curtain, which was pulled back to show the setup. An art storage and display area lined the far wall with a place for both framed and unframed prints, neatly organized with love.

She even added a worktable that sat by the window, providing natural light but with blinds in case I wanted to darken the room and work. I could already imagine what it would look like covered in my cutting mats or splashes of paint from some side projects. On one side of the worktable, there was a lightbox sitting beside a scanner, a place for negatives, and above it all, a hanging line to hold photos while drying. I could already see myself working here and, even more importantly, it felt like my space.

I could feel my eyes warming again as I turned and looked at Shana and my aunt. So, before I could start crying again, I blurted, "On to the next amazing space."

As I walked into my room, I couldn't control the tears this time. It was as if my aunt had peeked inside my head and found the plans for my dream home. I glanced at my aunt and Shana, who both had huge smiles mixed with a slight look of apprehension. I slowly moved further into the room and immediately fell in love with everything in there.

My happy tears had turned into blubbering at this point. I was overwhelmed at how much work, love, and understanding of me went into everything she'd done. I couldn't leave if I wanted to, and I didn't want to; I wanted to stay. Strange creatures or not, I was staying.

I turned back to look at my aunt again, and this time she knew. She knew I was going to stay with her. She and Shana made their way over to me, both wrapping me in a hug, as Aunt Ulla said, "Welcome home, Ash."

Shana, knowing how anxious I was, asked, "Are you *sure* you're going to stay?"

Aunt Ulla looked between us quizzically, "Why wouldn't you? Please tell me you did not get back with Richard."

Hurrying to calm my aunt, I said, "No, never. Richard is history. Dead and archived." I gave Shana a "not now" look, then continued, "How about I put my stuff in *my* room, and we get Shana settled, then we can sit and catch up until Mark gets here. Sound good?"

They both agreed, so my aunt took Shana to her and Mark's room as I finished putting my bags into my room.

I'd put work stuff in my office, and camera equipment in my studio, then sat on the edge of my bed and looked around the bedroom.

I think I'm going to get rid of most of the furniture in storage and keep all of this. The only things from storage I'll bring will be work items, a trunk I painted, a few sentimental pieces, and of course, my clothes. The rest I can donate.

I heard my name being called, so I ran downstairs to join the women in the kitchen. I got through the threshold to see my aunt was busy making coffee for us, so I asked her to sit down.

"There are a few things I want to ask you, Aunt Ulla..."

She looked concerned, so I reached over and patted her hand to reassure her that I was staying no matter what. Then I told her about everything that happened—my stop on the road to capture some scenery, the deer barreling out of the trees with the dogman chasing it, the dream from last night, how my car's trunk was scratched this morning, and then about the deer carcass.

I repeated that I was staying regardless of if there was a creature or not, "Who knows, it could be stress causing me to see things, or it might be Richard playing a nasty joke, I don't know, but I *do* know that I'm staying."

The look on her face said that she wasn't surprised, more concerned.

"Have you seen or heard anything strange up here?" I asked, "I mean, like, loud monstrous howling, strange screams, or maybe people saying they've seen Anubis or a werewolf walking around the woods?"

Aunt Ulla let out a deep sigh as she took my hands and said, "I have heard tales of something. But it's not my story to tell. You'll hear it soon enough. For now, it gets dark earlier up here, so let's make sure you've got everything out of your car and put it in the garage, okay?"

Feeling kind of shocked and not sure what to do, I decided to take the calm approach. I looked at Shana, then my aunt, and said, "Okay... then afterwards, can we get something to eat? Because I'm starving and I think it could be affecting my brain. Oh, Aunt Ulla, how's your Wi-Fi, internet connections, all that stuff up here?"

I smiled because I think she knew that would be one of my first questions.

She answered, "I had everything checked when the contractors were here. I had them make sure there was internet and anything else you might want or need for your computers, phones, and whatever else you may need the connection for. I had them check it several times before they left. You should be good to go, even if the snowstorm hits."

With that, we went back to my car, grabbed the last of our stuff, and I parked my car in one of the garages.

Shana and I took the rest of my stuff upstairs. She went to her room to get things put away as I started putting my clothes in the dresser and closet. I stopped briefly to look out the balcony door at the beautiful scene outside.

I could see across the lake from my room, and the view was spectacular. I had to blink several times, because I could have sworn I saw a large, black wolf staring at the lodge from the other side of the lake.

But when I looked again, it was gone.

Okay, so I may be seeing things.

I shook it off and decided to set up my computer in my office. I took my laptop and a box of office materials in and put them on the old desk. I logged onto my computer to check out the internet connection—it worked, and fast. I was surprised and impressed at the same time. After setting up my laptop, I decided to grab my tablet and join Shana and Aunt Ulla downstairs.

Aunt Ulla had set up some snacks, made each of us a tuna sandwich, and was coming out of the kitchen with sweet tea as I sat down. Setting my tablet aside, I jumped in and started eating. I kept the conversation light and fun. We all knew that things might get heavy soon, so we joked and reminisced over school memories and got caught up on each other's lives a little.

As we were just starting to get to the good stuff, Mark came in with arms full of grocery bags. Seeing that there was still food on the table, his face lit up at the prospect of lunch.

"I made it and, apparently, I have perfect timing because I'm hungry," he stated. "I still need to get the rest of the stuff out of the car. Mind giving me a hand, ladies?"

Shana and I followed him to help bring in the rest of the bags while Aunt Ulla made him a plate. As we brought everything in, Aunt Ulla put the food items away, then we all sat down to talk while we finished eating. Mark dug into his food like he hadn't eaten all day. While he was busy eating, I told Mark about the renovations and my amazing rooms—it was something he'd known about but was apparently good at keeping a secret.

Aunt Ulla chuckled, "Yes, Mark is very good at keeping secrets. Part of why I asked him to run some errands for me. One of the things I had him do was stop and talk to a good friend of mine about the things that have been going on around here. He's one of the mountain Elders. He knows about some of the happenings, and if he doesn't, one of the other Elders should. I think it would be good if you spoke with him about your, uh… incident."

Mark tried to talk while swallowing a mouthful, "I agree, Bidziil said something happened recently, but the Elders weren't sure how many of the dogmen were brought back. He said it could be anything from a relative of one of the dogmen warriors or an evil shaman that woke them. He also said it would have been an intensive ritual, and the council of Elders did not approve of any such rituals, ceremonies… anything. But he'll explain everything better when he gets here. He wanted to consult with a few of the other Elders first."

Hearing what Mark said made me wonder what was going on up here and why no one was talking about it. Feeling even more curious and confused, I realized I was in the middle of something much bigger than just being visited by a dogman in my sleep. Which reminded me that Mark didn't know about the dream yet, so I blurted out, "Maybe I should tell you about the dream I had last night."

Mark looked surprised but suggested that I wait until Bidziil got there. That way, I didn't have to repeat myself, and it shouldn't be too much longer.

We all fell quiet for a few minutes as we finished eating, and before I could say anything else, there was a knock on the door.

Mark jumped up, saying he'd get it, since we three ladies were laughing at ourselves for jumping at the knock like teenagers watching a scary movie. Mark came back and introduced the two older men with him. "Ladies, some of you know Bidziil, and this is Elder Tsali. We think Tsali might be able to help figure out what's up with the dogman. Tsali is one of the key council members and the keeper of their ways, so he knows more of their lore and history."

Bidziil and Tsali waved hello, while Aunt Ulla motioned for them to have a seat. Both sat on the bench at the table, but I noticed that Bidziil made sure to sit as close as possible to Aunt Ulla, and they shared a smile that I noticed lingered just a bit longer than necessary for a hello.

Mark went on to say he had informed them about the event yesterday and the gift from this morning, and then asked me to share the dream I had mentioned.

I stood up and began to pace as I retold the dream, ending with, "And something else... I think I saw it across the lake earlier. Strangely, it seems like every time I talk or think about the creature, it's weird, but almost like there's a connection of sorts that—I don't know—I can feel its touch again." I raised my hand and touched my cheek, feeling the spot where the dogman had touched me. Tingles shot to my core as I remembered his touch and the rumble of his deep voice. As I let out a deep breath. Apparently, I was deeper in thought than I realized because Shana cleared her throat to get my attention.

"Um, sorry. Well, that's all," I finished.

Tsali stood up and then guided me to sit down on the couch in the living room. He sat down across from me on the coffee table, took my hands, closed his eyes, and began a chant. The others followed us into the living room and stood on the other side of the room watching. We all looked at Mark and Bidziil. Mark shrugged his shoulders and whispered, "Just go with it."

After a couple of minutes, Tsali opened his eyes, smiled, stood up, and asked to talk with Mark and Bidziil privately. They stepped into the library. Far enough, I couldn't hear them, but I could still see them through the glass doors, whispering and motioning to me. It all seemed so strange, but they came back to the living room within a few minutes, and Tsali spoke, "I will explain the lore of the creature and what may be going on."

He kept me in his main line of sight while talking to all of us.

He began slowly, "In ancient times, we were protected by warriors who took a vow to be of service to the native people of the mountain. Outsiders later called them dogmen or creatures, but among the mountain tribes, they were known as the Guardian Night Warriors. The tribe's Elders chose two warriors from each of the four mountain tribes. After completing many tests and trials, they would be considered Guardian Night Warriors. They were transformed into wolf creatures that nightly roamed through these woods, deterring strangers from settling here or destroying sacred places on the mountain. The people of the mountain clans were extremely grateful and blessed the warriors with immortality, the strength of ten bears, the sight of an eagle, the agility of the mountain lion, and the cunning of the wolf. Most do not know that the ritual was given to one of the Ancients in a dream where he was contacted by a member of the White Brotherhood—who were great spiritual ancestors. During the dream, he was told these warriors would protect the mountain and her people as long as they did not wage war against each other. If there were a war, the Dog Gods would not return to human form. They must wait for two hundred years and then undergo another, more extensive ritual before regaining their human forms. He was then given the ritual to create the warriors. He was also warned that, if he was to create them, he would need to give a worthy offering or else there would be a sacrifice of some sort to either him or the tribes. After the ritual was completed, they would take on the appearance of a

Dog God at night and return to their human forms during the day. Unless he did not heed the warnings."

He looked directly at me and added with a half-smile, "Like you described the Egyptian God, Anubis, but with more of a wolf appearance. Anyway, they are immortal, and even though there was a war, they watched over the people and the mountain. If all went well then after serving one hundred years, the White Brotherhood decided they would be gifted an opportunity to find their true mates, and to return to their human forms. Until they find their mates, they can only appear as humans through dreams or to the Elders in visions with messages. History then tells of the war that broke out among the tribes and, as a result, the native people lost the mountain to outsiders. The Elders performed a ritual to call the Guardian Night Warriors back, sending them to the sleep realm so that the tribes would not use them for evil against one another. But more importantly, so the outsiders could not learn of them, torture them, or worse, control them. They were to sleep until they were called upon once more to protect all tribes and the mountain."

Tsali took a deep breath, sighed, looked around at everyone, and then back to me.

"So, it seems you have found one of the Guardian Night Warriors. A few months ago, I, too, saw one of the warriors in the woods... and he was aware of me. Later that night, he came to me in a dream, angry and asked why he was called out of the sleep realm when there was no peace among the people, and the mountain belonged to the outsiders. He wanted to know about this time period. I promised to find out what I could as quickly as possible and suggested he stay out of sight, since there are hunters and others who would like to try to kill him, or worse. Last night, he returned and asked me to search for you. He sensed a connection—especially after smelling you. He did mention leaving you a gift."

He smiled slightly as he said this, because I'm sure he knew what the so-called gift was.

I had mixed feelings about what Tsali told me. I was scared, yet curious and intrigued, not to mention kind of flattered, in a strange way.

Speaking directly to Tsali, I snorted, "A gift? He left me a dead deer. That is not a gift—at least not for me–flowers maybe, but not a dead deer. Look, I love dogs, don't get me wrong, but... seriously?"

I took a breath to calm myself before continuing, "What I want to know is how and why he woke up? Why is he curious about me? What did I do for this, OH, and what's wrong with the way I smell? I didn't have perfume on, and my deodorant has no scent, so is he saying I stunk? Like he has room to talk—he smelled all musky, wild, and a little like a wet dog."

I took another deep breath since I slipped into a slight rant. And I could see the others trying to hold back a laugh while Tsali smiled and thoughtfully said, "The other Elders and I, we have a lead on who woke him, and this person needs to be caught before they wake all of the Night Warriors. There are others who are awake as well. We must find a way to keep this person from using them for evil. We are unsure of the exact number of original warriors that were created, and only a guess of how many that may have been awakened. The Elders are doing as much as possible to find out as much as they can before things get any worse. We do feel it is only three warriors that were brought back from slumber. Please believe me, Ms. Ashley, when I say there has always been a kind of evil on this mountain, and it has only grown in strength since the mining companies came here.

The first group of miners showed up on the mountain in the 1800s. At first, they started with pickaxes and shovels, staying in the low stream areas. Digging tunnels that were dark and dangerous. Men were paid low wages and were not treated kindly by the companies. Many men died in those tunnels. Then the machines were brought in, and the mountain has been dying twice as fast ever since. Death is a natural part of life, but when mankind becomes involved... nature often takes on a twisted, unnatural existence, and then death is not far behind. This death energy has fed the evil.

Fortunately, many have left, but the heart of the evil remains and that seems to have fueled the energy that brought the warriors out of slumber. Since we do not know for sure if your dogman was the first to wake up, he and the other two will be our first point of focus. Now, we know that the owner of the main mining company has been trying to buy every property he can. He has scared several into selling at a low amount, but there are quite a few that are holding out— thanks to your aunt. He can't do anything if she doesn't sell to him. It is possible that he had something to do with the warriors being brought back, but he has not shown up in the vision work we have been doing."

Unfortunately, connecting the man in question with this has been hard to prove. The resurrector has stayed one step ahead of us, in the shadows. When Bidziil called me, I knew I had to come and speak with you. The warrior's name is easy enough to say, even though it is of the old language, it is based on Cherokee. He is Wahaya, Chief of the Guardian Night Warriors. I thought you should know, instead of calling him a creature or a dogman. Knowing his name and who he was... might help you to see past his teeth and into his soul. He is more than what you've seen. Shortly after he came to me the first time, I went to the ancestors and petitioned for information about the dog warriors. They were known by some of the mountain tribe members as Guardian Night Warriors. Anyway, after getting approval and guidance, they shared that they knew of this warrior, his history, and that he had been in a slumber for over two hundred years. He was the original Ancient Warrior turned Dog God or Guardian Night Warrior. Even before the ceremony, he was respected and loved by his fellow warriors and the tribes. He was fair even with their enemies. Wahaya gave his all for his people and even the other tribes. He was loved, trusted, and respected. It is said he was born to be a leader who would bring all tribes together. When he agreed to go through the ceremony,... the other warriors and the Ancestors agreed he would be their Chief. But back to the evil one. As I said earlier, the one who has summoned them is staying in the shadows. It is unknown what this person wants with the warriors. The other two warriors have not been spotted... yet. Wahaya, your dogman, and I are concerned about what is going on. He has sensed the other two, but they are staying away from him. If the others are running loose in the mountains as Wahaya was, or depending on who's controlling them, there could be human casualties. Luckily, Wahaya does not seem to be under the control of the evil one."

I could see Tsali weighing his response before speaking. He looked deeply into my eyes before he said, "He truly is more than what you have seen. He has a soul and is a warrior of the Ancients. His curiosity about you is not to be seen as fearful. He feels he has known you before in his human life. Wahaya also said he will protect you if there is evil or if others try to come around. He will protect all of you, and his tribe, which is now only a few of us who have stayed on the mountain. He hopes you will look beyond this image of him."

I glanced around at everyone as I took in yet another deep breath, "I don't know... I can try. But right now, I'm a bit freaked out. I mean—this is right out of a horror movie. My life is in flux, and I'm trying to get back on track with my life. I don't see myself being ready for anything for awhile, plus frankly, a dogman... that is fucked up. Excuse my language, but it is."

As I stood up, I looked to Tsali, "Look, Tsali, I'm sorry, but I'm in the dark as to what is going on with the mining—and as far as having a dogman protecting me, that's nice and all, I guess, but it doesn't answer my questions. I need to do some processing... Aunt Ulla, Shana, everyone, I think I'm going to head upstairs, finish unpacking, decompress, and try to forget what is going on for at least an hour. I'll be back down in a bit to help prepare for the storm, but right now... I need some alone time."

Aunt Ulla then got up, making sure to walk Tsali and Bidziil out. I noticed she walked really close to Bidziil and even touched his arm a few times. I smiled on my way upstairs.

Once I made it to my room, I headed to the balcony, which used to be one of my favorite places to hang out when I was little. As I stood at the railing, I was able to see Aunt Ulla talking to Bidziil, and that Tsali was already in the truck. As I watched them, there seemed to be a sweetness in how they talked and smiled at each other, then Bidziil opened the driver's door to leave. But before he got in, he kissed Aunt Ulla on the cheek, and they hugged. It seemed to be a little more than a friendly hug; there was a deeper warmth to it, but I could be wrong. If I'm not—more power to them. Once Bidziil and Tsali left, Aunt Ulla came back inside, then Mark and Shana went out and brought some firewood in from the shed to put under the back deck of the house.

The balcony outside my little apartment had the best view of the lodge. Not only could I see part of the driveway, but I had an amazing view of the mountains, lake, and the sky without any man-made disruptions to its beauty. I still couldn't believe how amazing it was to have over half of the top floor of the lodge. It seems to have grown since I've been gone.

Apparently, Aunt Ulla expanded the lodge somewhat and even had an elevator put in and moved her bedroom upstairs. So, the top floor had my wing, my aunt's room, a guest room, and an inside elevator. The main floor consisted of the lounge, library, dining room, kitchen, a mudroom, four more guest rooms, and then a closed-in sun deck. Surprisingly, the lodge also had a basement, which was turned into a game room with a pool table, darts, and a small bar area. Two storage rooms and the laundry room were also located in the basement, and thankfully, the elevator went down that far.

Aunt Ulla had added two cabins and another barn to the property since I was last here. So much has changed in the last six years. I may have only been with Richard for three, but between school, work, traveling, and him, I was MIA from the lodge a majority of that time. After mom died, visiting was full of happy memories I didn't want to change or sad ones that were too painful to feel.

My thoughts shifted to deep reflections of the last 48 hours. Suddenly, I was pulled out of my thoughts as a feeling came over me, and my eyes found a patch of trees on the other side of the lake.

There he was—a faint dark silhouette. Wahaya, my Anubis or dogman.

Chapter 4

I could tell he was watching me, even though I couldn't make out his expression, he stayed mostly in the shadows. I knew it was him... because I felt him. I could sense his emotions. So much came through the invisible connection we had... fear of rejection, longing, and sadness.

As he watched me, I knew he felt my apprehension and fear. He lowered his head, then turned, slowly walking deeper into the darkness of the forest. I felt a tear roll down my cheek as I turned to go back inside.

It hadn't been long, maybe thirty minutes, when I made my way back downstairs. I had been upstairs a little longer than anticipated, and I guess I got caught up in the view.

Once in the kitchen, I jumped in to help Aunt Ulla finish filling water jugs and making sure the back-up generators were in good condition with oil and fuel.

After we finished with the outside work, she started putting some of the extra stuff away that Mark had brought. Once we were done with those chores, we made sure our bedrooms had extra blankets, candles, a jug or two of water, flashlights with extra batteries, and then made sure the oil lanterns were ready in case we needed them too.

Aunt Ulla thought of everything and had Mark pick up quite a bit of fuel, non-perishable food items, toilet paper, paper towels, two coolers with several bags of ice in them— not that we'll need ice when we could use snow, which, there's supposed to be plenty of—but hey who am I to question when I hadn't been in a bad snowstorm since I was little? It looked like there was enough to last several months for at least four, maybe even six, people.

By the time we finished making sure the lodge was ready, we were all tired and hungry. I always wondered why she kept such a large place after Uncle Carl died, but she said the reason they bought it in the first place was to get far away from the city and open a place where others could come take a breath, get away from the noise, pollution, and rat race of the large cities—a type of sanctuary.

Since they never had children, they wanted to share the peace with anyone willing to "just be," as Uncle Carl would say. Now she was finally able to fulfil their dream, although, sadly, without him. Uncle Carl died in a car accident on the way back from the place they wanted to get away from—the big city.

He'd gone to Louisville, Kentucky for his last work trip before he retired. He had to turn in a few things and pick up a surprise gift for Aunt Ulla and the lodge. He'd gotten them matching jackets made with the lodge name and emblem on them as well as a front door emblem and welcome mat to match.

It was his last trip to town for work, so he decided to pick them up, putting him behind leaving the city before a torrential rainstorm hit. He wasn't able to beat the storm, and we were told he was swept off the road into an overflowing creek. Somehow his car ended up-side-down.

The police weren't sure what happened first —he may have had a heart attack and lost control, and that was why his car was swept into the creek so quickly, or his heart attack was caused by the fear of losing control. Either way, we lost him that day. He and Aunt Ulla had finished building a few cabins and were going to open the lodge to visitors after his retirement party, which was within a month, when the accident happened. After the funeral, she almost sold the lodge, but said she couldn't because he was here.

She wanted the lodge as much as he did, and she couldn't let his, *their*, dream die. They both had put so much of themselves in the lodge; his spirit was in this place. So, she kept it and continued to renovate it. The money from his life insurance, money from her art sales, and their inheritance kept things running. She was able to make all the improvements they had talked about. Mom and I would come stay with Aunt Ulla, sometimes for a month or more. Then, when mom started getting sick, we would only do short visits. Aunt Ulla offered for us to move in with her, but Mom needed to be closer to the hospitals. After my mother—Uncle Carl's sister—had died of cancer, visits to the lodge were few. I kept my head down, studied, got my degree, and then I was working and stayed away.

I visited twice while I was in school, and once with Richard, because I wanted to reconnect with my aunt. We did get to reconnect somewhat, but Richard didn't like her, or coming to the lodge. He was not an outdoorsy kind of guy and hated the mountains. I should have known there was something wrong with him then and dropped him like a hot potato. But no, it was still early on in our relationship. So, my aunt and I would only talk over the phone while he was out. I can't believe I gave up my family and mountain beauty for him.

God, I was stupid.

I can't believe I've been gone for so long; I'd forgotten how beautiful it was out here and how great it is to have a natural quiet that's only interrupted by nature's sounds. I love it, and I'm still kicking myself for not coming to visit more, but I'm home now.

Realizing I went off on one of my memory excursions again, I reeled myself in and finished putting the blanket, flashlight, and batteries in my closet when my stomach growled.

My stomach growled again, and I remembered that we still needed to eat dinner and clean up. I made my way downstairs to see Aunt Ulla, Shana, and Mark walking into the kitchen. Upon seeing them, I quickly blurted out, "So, how about we all get cleaned up and then I'll cook, sound good?"

Aunt Ulla turned around to face me and said, "Well, how about Shana and Mark get cleaned up first, and I'll wait until after dinner to shower. Ash, would you be okay with helping me start dinner and then maybe take a hot shower right before bed to help you sleep? I made your favorite tiramisu this morning. We can have it for dessert."

Once I heard 'tiramisu,' I was already halfway through the kitchen door as she finished saying dessert.

"If you get started on the garlic bread and spaghetti, I'll make my special meatballs. Plus, I have some homemade sauce in the fridge. Is that okay with everyone?" Aunt Ulla asked.

As all four of us nodded our heads 'yes' in hungry agreement, I added, "Yeah, I think that's an even better idea. Plus, it will give us time to catch up—Aunt Ulla, you can tell me how long you've been dating Bidziil." I smiled as I gave my aunt a side-eye wink and saw a blush seep into her cheeks.

As Mark was leaving, he spoke up, "I'm in, but please make extra garlic bread. I love me some garlic bread, a few pieces with cheese too."

Laughing, Shana swatted his butt before he could make another request, "You don't need all that cheese or bread, and I'm sure there'll be plenty. You're such a carb guy... now go."

Looking back at us, she said, "You'd think he'd weigh three hundred pounds the way he eats—instead, I gain it for him!"

We all laughed while Shana and Mark continued to their room. Aunt Ulla and I worked in a long-missed unison as we started getting everything together for dinner.

I paused for a moment, gathering my thoughts and words, before saying, "Aunt Ulla, I'm sorry. I didn't mean to stay away so long. I should have been here for you and let you be there for me when mom passed. Instead, I closed myself off. Then the whole thing with Richard. I'm so... so sorry."

I started to tear up and couldn't get the next words out before my aunt came to hug me. Her warm smile let me know everything was okay and she replied, "Sweetheart, I knew you'd come home when you were ready. Yes, I would have loved to be there for you, but I didn't want to push. Shana kept me updated on how and what you were doing. If you needed me, I was here for you or I would have been by your side at the first SOS call. I knew you'd be okay, maybe a bit bruised, but okay. So, no regrets... you hear me?"

I wiped my eyes, "Yes, and one last serious thing before we have no more serious talks for the night—and that includes talking about strange creatures—okay?" I gave her a quick hug, then continued, "I love you, Aunt Ulla, and I am *so* glad to be home ... I absolutely LOVE my section of the lodge! It was like you were in my head. Thank you so much, it's perfect!"

Starting to tear up again, I pulled away, "Now, we should probably make extra food and put it in the back of the fridge, so we have leftovers. With Mark around, I'm not so sure there'll be any left if we don't."

We both chuckled and I remembered how much fun it was to be here and cook with my mom and aunt when I was little after my dad left us—and then through my teenage years, and after Uncle Carl passed. I smiled at the heart-warming memories, took a deep breath and began making one of my favorite meals.

Aunt Ulla and I continued to make small talk while we moved about the kitchen, each with our task in hand. And before you know it, the kitchen smelled like an Italian eatery. Aunt Ulla admitted that she and Bidziil have been seeing each other for a few months, but that she feels a bit guilty because of Uncle Carl. I let her know that he would have wanted the best for her, and she'd been alone long enough.

We heard Mark and Shana coming down the stairs, so Aunt Ulla changed the subject to dinner just as they came bounding through the door. They came in time to set the table, and we all agreed on no more serious talk for tonight. I reminded Mark, no *dogman* conversations either. I know we'll have to talk about him at some point, but not tonight.

We did go over a few stories of snowstorms and the silly things people, mainly Mark, did during them. Then, after dinner dishes had been cleaned, Aunt Ulla went up to shower while we watched the news. When she came back, we had some hot cocoa with marshmallows and tiramisu. By the time we were done having dessert and cleaning up again, I was ready to drop into a deep coma-like sleep, silently hoping I wouldn't have an intruder in my dreams- or maybe I did want to see him again? Especially now that I know his story. I watched as Shana and Mark got up and said goodnight, then

Aunt Ulla said she was headed to bed too and asked if I needed anything.

"Thank you, Aunt Ulla, but if I do need anything I can get it myself. Now that I live here, I want to be useful, and you don't have to treat me like a guest. I'm currently debating whether to make another hot chocolate—with or without a shot of bourbon. I was thinking it might make sure I sleep soundly."

She smiled, "And to sleep through any possible visits from Mr. Anubis."

I smiled back with a half laugh, "Exactly! I have a lot to think about, with the move, my job, the breakup. I need to clear my head and figure out what I want to focus on first. He may have been asleep for a few hundred years, but I haven't, and I want some down time to think and take photos, and just be. Ya' know?"

Aunt Ulla walked over and gave me a hug, "Yes, I do. Been there. You do what's right for you, sweetheart. Things will work out as they should. Now, I'm going to bed. I have to be up extra early in the morning to feed the chickens and check on the horses. I know Mark said he'd take care of them, but they're my big babies. Goodnight, Ash, love you, sweetheart."

"Goodnight, Aunt Ulla, love you and sweet dreams."

I heard the elevator go up as I made my way back to the kitchen. And even though it's not a ton of stairs, I may have to take the elevator too, since I felt sore from the days' work.

Hmm, maybe I'll make a hot toddy instead of hot chocolate, which will definitely put me to sleep.

I found some decaf blackberry tea and blackberry honey, which I'm pretty sure Aunt Ulla made. I added a squeeze of lemon, and a little whiskey—okay, a bit more than a little. I'm not much of a whiskey drinker, but I'd try almost anything to help me fall into a deep sleep for the night. Taking my drink upstairs, slowly sipping as I rode the elevator, I felt the warmth slowly consuming me from my head to my toes. Once I reached my apartment, I closed the curtains and headed for the shower.

My shower was longer than usual, but the hot water cascading over my sore muscles felt so soothing. I had to force myself to get out, especially when the cool air hit my body. I toweled off quickly, got dressed, and finished drinking my now cold sleep concoction. The whiskey's burn spread into a slow internal heat, which I hoped would help me sleep.

Before crawling into bed, I peeked out the curtains, trying to scan the darkness for any signs of Mr. Anubis, as I had jokingly called him, but I didn't see or even sense him. A slight feeling of disappointment washed over me, and I tried to shake it off. I slipped under the huge, fluffy comforter with a thick faux fur blanket on top. The sheets were cold, but a good cold. With the weight of the blankets, the hot shower, and the hot toddy, I felt myself slipping fast into a deep sleep.

~

Wahaya

I stepped out from behind a tree moments after I saw that her light went out. I knew she had entered dreamtime now. My human side wanted to give her time to feel our connection, while inside does not have time to wait or waste. I was torn between going to her or staying away.

My human half spoke quietly, "Our soul recognizes her, and we have a connection, but she must feel it for herself. We will not force her. With heightened senses, I smell her, feel her, sense her emotions, even in sleep, and I long for her. My love—she is internally conflicted. There is fear, sorrow, and longing within her heart. I will let her sleep tonight; her heart will give her dreams tonight, not I. But I will visit her again soon, very soon."

I then turned to go deeper into the forest and sent a whisper to her heart...

ZᎧb TBᴔᎫ dᎦMУ OᴗZ Dh ᴔᏆᎾᴔᎫ TᏚ dhᏑRᴔУ

May the stars weave gentle dreams around your heart.

ᏋᎯ hLᴂᎧᏋ DhᏚᎧᏋ OᴗᎦᴔᎫ DᏝᏐᎦᎫ

You are my soul's eternal love.

~

Ash

I woke up with a start, feeling a type of ache and sadness. I sat up and grabbed my phone to check the time—3:00 a.m. and no Anubis. I was a bit disappointed there was no visit or dream, and that the hot toddy didn't knock me out for the full night.

As I got up to go to the bathroom, I felt an urge to go out on the balcony. I forced myself to go straight to the bathroom instead, but when I came back, my body took over. The next thing I knew, I was standing outside looking across the lake. Strangely, I wanted to see him. Maybe to prove that I wasn't crazy, but then again, there felt like a deeper reason I couldn't quite reach yet.

The night sky was lighter than usual, since the storm was close, and a few flakes of snow had begun to fall. The moon aided the snow by lighting up the lake and the area at the edge of the forest. I thought I saw a shadow there, but it was late, so my eyes were probably blurry. I stood in a cloud of emotional confusion and waited for a sign that he was there watching me, but... nothing.

As I turned to go back in, I sent up a silent prayer to the mountain to guide me in understanding what was going on and why. Uncle Carl once told me that the mountain was wise and held secrets that only it, and God, could know. He also said that if I was perplexed and it had to do with the mountain or its people, to pray and ask for answers. This was my first time asking, but I definitely needed help.

I walked back to my bed as I spoke to the ceiling, "Uncle Carl, maybe you and the mountain can shed some light and help me to understand what part I play in this mess. Because right now I'm at a loss." As I laid down, I could swear I heard a low hum—almost like the mountain itself was breathing— and I drifted off to a dreamless sleep.

Chapter 5

Whoever invented the alarm was sadistic. And why I set an alarm for today was beyond me, but I did. Then I remembered I wanted to help Aunt Ulla and Mark with the animals. I dragged myself out of bed and remembered my 3:00 a.m. plea for clarity from my uncle and the mountain, glad that no one knew about it yet. They would think I'm even crazier for talking to a mountain and a dead person.

Geez, I'm messed up.

My backup alarm went off, and I hurried to get ready before running downstairs.

Aunt Ulla, Mark, and Shana were putting on their coats and were almost at the back door as I hit the bottom step. "Are you all heading out already?"

Aunt Ulla replied, saying, "Honey, the snow was worse than anticipated, and we need to make sure the animals are fed and that the barn heater is working. This is the first time since last winter that we've had to turn it on other than to test it out. We also need to double-check the generators. We covered them, but it looks like the tarps flew off. Instead of coming with us, would you mind starting breakfast? Make it a big one because after we're done, we'll be hungry, and Bidziil is on his way to help too. He's bringing more supplies, and his grandson Adohi, so set for at least six. They'll be staying for a few days too. Bidziil said Adohi is staying with him while his mother is on a work retreat, and she thought it would be a good time for him to learn the old ways. So, it looks like he'll get a crash course in storm prepping. The storm is supposed to get even worse, so it could be at least a week before anyone can leave."

"Wow, when I was up at three, it seemed like it was just starting to snow. All this happened in just a few hours?" I looked out the window to see over a foot of snow on the ground.

"How is he going to get up here? That's a lot of snow, and you said there's more on the way? Mark, what about you—don't you have to be back at work?"

As he opened the back door, Mark replied, "I had already let work know where I was going and that if I couldn't get back for a while, my second, Michael, was to keep in contact and be in charge. Bidziil has a snow-truck with some special additives put on it, so it's nothing for him to make it during a snowstorm. In fact, he and a few of the other Elders are often the ones people up here call for help, not the police. So, he'll be okay to get up here. Bidziil wants to be here for Aunt Ulla, especially since this is to be one hell of a storm, which is why he's planning on staying."

Mark handed me something right before he headed out, "Here's a walkie-talkie, we all have one in case we need help or something. We'll let you know when we're heading back in. See you soon. Oh, and Ash, really strong coffee, please."

Then they were out the door, and it was almost as if they disappeared. The snow shielded them against me until my eyes focused, then I could see three darkish blurs moving toward the barn.

I headed into the kitchen to get everything out and start on breakfast. I decided to make homemade biscuits and gravy with bacon, eggs, and vegetables. After getting all the ingredients together, I put on two pots of coffee. One strong enough that it could walk on its own, one bold and aromatic with a hazelnut flavor for us girls, or those who hoped to sleep within the next twenty-four hours. Once the coffees were brewing, I started on the biscuits and made sure to make extra. If there were any left over, we could have them tomorrow or feed the birds as a treat. I knew Aunt Ulla had bird food she put out, but a treat every now and then can't hurt, especially in this weather, poor things.

Thinking about the birds made me think about other animals freezing in the snow, and then my heart sank. What about Wahaya?

Where would he go? How would he stay warm? Does he even get cold? I would think he does, since he's come out of the dream world. Maybe I'll leave him a plate of food out and a blanket or two.

I realized I was worrying over a dangerous creature, so I decided to turn on the radio for a little music to cook to, and then got back to cooking.

I prepared the big dining table with six settings and took the last batch of biscuits out of the oven. Then I stopped for a cup of coffee before I started on the eggs, when there was a loud knock on the back door. I jumped and spilled my coffee.

"Well, shit. Coming!" I shouted as I hurried to clean myself up while moving to the door. I flung it open to see five very cold people with bags in their arms trying to shuffle in. Bidzill must have pulled around back to unload supplies. Aunt Ulla and Shana came in first and headed into the pantry while Mark, Bidziil, and his grandson went downstairs to the storage area. I could swear I heard teeth chattering. I closed and locked the door behind them, then ran to the kitchen to finish the eggs and get all the food on the table.

The ladies came back first. They took their coats off and immediately went for the food. Shortly after they sat, they were joined by the men. Bidziil introduced me to his grandson

Adohi. Nice looking kid, maybe around 19 years old. His eyes told me he was wise beyond his years, then he spoke...

"After we eat, is there Wi-Fi or something? I started this new game, and I really want to finish the first level."

And... Wisdom took a back seat to a game.

We all settled and dug into the food with very little talking—except for going over the snowstorm, what to do, and what not to do.

Once everyone was done eating, the men headed back outside to shovel a walkway from the house to the barn and coop. Shana, Aunt Ulla, and I started the cleanup from breakfast, and Aunt Ulla explained that it will be easier to keep the paths clean if we keep shoveling them every few hours. We also had a snowblower that one of the guys was using.

Once everyone was done, we all settled near the fireplace. I hung out for a few minutes, then decided to go upstairs. I let everyone know I was going to do a little work and that if they needed me, they could use the walkie-talkie instead of coming up, because it would be more fun.

First, I went to the kitchen and grabbed a huge mug of coffee, which would last me a few hours, then went to head upstairs. However, Shana caught me and asked if she could look at my photos from the past few days. I knew she wanted to see how the footprint photo came out and to ask if I had any dreams. So, I had to say yes, and we both headed up to my studio.

As Shana and I walked up the stairs, she said, "Your aunt did a great job with the studio. I think she thought of everything, and the darkroom is top-notch."

"Yeah, I'm still in awe of all that she did. I spent a little time in there yesterday getting a few things ready to work on."

With a slightly sheepish voice, Shana asked, "So, did you have any dreams last night?"

"Wow, not beating around the bush, are you?" I asked, laughing. "No, I didn't have any dreams, but I did wake up at 3 a.m. to pee. Strangely enough, I was hoping for a dream for some reason. I don't know what's wrong with me, but I feel something like a weird connection to it."

"Ash, it's not weird. Mark and I were talking, and it could be possible that the connection you have is from your ancestors. I know your aunt isn't from here, but didn't you tell me once that your mom and dad's family were from this area, and that's why your uncle wanted the lodge here? I mean, who knows? Maybe you and this creature were together before Wahaya became a dogman. That could explain the connection, right?"

I stopped for a moment, then hesitantly told her about seeing him at the edge of the trees and the empathic feelings I was having, not to forget the regret of not having a dream.

"I know it's strange, and this is, like, so fucking quick. If there is some sort of connection, I need to know why, and even if there is—what does he think is going to happen? It's not like I could be in a relationship with it. One kiss and my face would be gone."

At that, we both broke out into laughter.

"Wow, Ash, not a good image at all. But seriously—are you avoiding finding out about the connection because of Richard, maybe?"

I thought about what she said for a moment, did a quick emotional soul search, and answered her honestly, "No, I'm not. Richard and I haven't really had a relationship for the last year—hell, we hadn't had sex in the last six months. I thought it was because of me and my schedule, but I came to find out he had been getting it elsewhere for over a year, or more, who truly knows. There was no love lost there.

"No, I think if I really look deep, I'm scared to make a connection because if he is, let's say the one, how could I be with a creature? And if he were to turn into a human, would he then die, or, I don't know, lose the link to us? I'm really confused, like I said, I prayed to the mountain and my dead uncle, so you know I need help. Anyway, I want him to come tonight—I have questions. Hell, if I thought he'd come now, I'd take a nap. Oh, and I was thinking, you know how we put extra bird seed out during the winter, throw out hay, and some cat food for the other animals—do you think he'll be okay in the snowstorm? If he's been in a dreamworld or cave for hundreds of years, he may not be ready for this storm. I thought about putting some blankets and food over on the side of the lake where I saw him. Do you think that's crazy?"

"Yes, Ash, that is crazy, but I agree. How about before it gets dark, you and I take some blankets and food out there? Mark could come with us to help carry stuff, not to mention, protect us. So, while you get some rest, I'm going to head downstairs and ask your aunt to make some food, so your Wahaya doesn't go hungry and wants to eat us instead. Oh, and I'll grab a few extra blankets from storage. Now, take a nap. You were up early."

"Thank you! After I finish checking these negatives, I just might lie down for a few. Who knows, maybe Uncle Carl or the mountain might answer me," I said in a kind of half laugh.

Shana got up to leave and told me to sleep tight as she closed the door. I looked at the negatives from my shots on the mountain, and there, in plain view, is guess who—the dogman, Wahaya. I looked closer, taking in every inch of him. I had to admit, he is a predator machine.   His fur was an obsidian black with a sheen bestowed by the Gods; his feet and hands looked almost human, except for the huge claws. His arms and legs were pure muscle and power. As I looked at his chest muscles, I had a strange desire to run my hands through his fur; his chest was wide and commanding. He could give any Greek God a run for their money. And his lower region, well, he was quite virile and uninhibited. I had to look away.

Was there something wrong with me? Because I started to feel a bit heated... I put the negatives and my equipment away and walked back to my room. I pulled one of the extra faux fur blankets down and set it in a chair, then, for some strange reason, I took off my clothes, lay down, and wrapped myself in the blanket on my bed. As I drifted off, I thought that I wanted him to have this blanket because it had my smell on it. I wasn't sure why, but I wanted him to fall asleep being able to smell my scent.

~

Later, I awoke to Shana knocking on my door, "Ash, honey, are you okay? You've been asleep for several hours, and it'll be getting dark soon."

Stretching as I sat up, I took a moment to orient myself after such a long nap. I yelled back to Shana, "Oh wow! Sorry, I guess I really needed that nap. And before you ask, no there were no dreams. I'll be down in a few minutes after I put on some warmer clothes."

I heard her go back down the steps and I hurried to get on some warmer clothes. I threw on my winter boots and grabbed the blanket.

I made it downstairs, and everyone looked at me immediately. Aunt Ulla spoke up first. "Are you sure you want to do this? Shana told us what you were thinking and—are you sure?"

Bidziil added, "If you do this, he may see this as an invitation of sorts."

Mark then spoke up, "Yeah, this might not be a good idea, but if you are going to do it, then we need to get going, now."

I looked at all of them as I nodded my head and said, "I know he may think this is an invite, or whatever, and, who knows, maybe it is? I'm not sure how I feel right now. But I do know that I can't let him possibly freeze or kill something or someone to be able to eat. Aunt Ulla, you may remember I have a hard time thinking of anything dying, and I'm not going to start with him, regardless of what he, or it, is."

I turned to Mark and Shana, then stated, "Shana, why don't you stay here? That way, it's only the two of us out there. He might be more threatened if he saw there were three of us. We'll be okay. Mark, let's go, it's starting to get dark."

Shana thought for a moment, then replied, "He also might see Mark as a threat or rival. How about you and I go? I've used an auger before, and Mark, before you say anything, I'll also take your shotgun. You can also watch us from the back. We will be fine, I trust Ash's instincts, and she feels things will be fine. So, I'll go instead."

Mark started to argue, but Shana kissed him to stop any further discussion, then walked over and picked up the shotgun, and headed out the door, grabbing her coat on the way.

Mark and I looked at each other, then grabbed the box of food, blankets, and the metal rod and auger to drill a hole in the lake so the animals could get water. I put on my coat and then wrapped myself in the blanket I was going to give Wayaha. I kept thinking the more it smelled like me, the better.

As Shana and I climbed into the UTV, Mark looked at us seriously, then said, "Ash, are you sure you want to do this? If he attacks you two, I won't be able to get to you fast enough." Switching to his comical self, he added, "I may be a strong, sexy, gun-toting sheriff, and one of your best friends, but I can only run so fast, and my shotgun isn't going to be enough to help either of you."

Without thinking, I said, "He won't hurt me, so if he does come at us... Shana can run. I feel that I'd be fine. But I don't think he will show. If he is there, he'll stay hidden."

Without saying anything else, Mark smiled, reluctantly acknowledged us with a nod, then kissed Shana a quick goodbye and stepped back so we could leave. Shana started the motor, and off we went with a slight jerk of the UTV.

The hum of the motor was the only noise we heard as we made our way to the other side of the lake. Once we got to the clearing, Shana jumped out, leaving the motor going, and looked at me, "Last time, I promise... Are you sure? You know animals can survive on snow when they're thirsty, right?"

"Yes," I replied, "I want to do this. It's the right thing. Plus, there are so many animals that will be happy with fresh water. What can I help with?"

Shana grabbed the rod and auger and said, "Let's get this done as quickly as possible and make sure nothing comes out to get us. The shotgun is in the back in case your friend gets a little eager. It won't kill him, but it might give us a head start to get away. Might! Help me get the ice holes started, and then you keep watch."

Shana finished with the lake, and then we drove to the tree line. She made sure to turn the UTV towards the lodge, so all we had to do was drop the stuff and go. We took the plastic tub of cooked meats and vegetables out and set it near the tree I pointed to, and then I put the blankets on top.

As we walked back to the UTV, I looked to the woods, and though I didn't see him, I felt his presence. Wahaya was there. I tried to speak so only he could hear me, "I thought you might need some food and blankets since you haven't been out of the dream world for a while, and it's supposed to be really bad for the next couple of nights, if not longer. There's food in the tub, if you like it, maybe bring the tub back, and I'll fill it up again, if I can. The blankets are for you, too. I hope you have a cave or somewhere dry to stay. I've brought you several, plus... one of mine. For some reason, I thought you might like that one. It's this one." I picked it up and rubbed the fur across my cheek, "I hope they help. Stay safe, Wahaya."

As I turned and walked back to the UTV, I heard a deep, dark voice in my head, "ᏩᏙ ᎠᏞᏆᏩᏗ ᎠᏂᏍᏬ."

As I climbed into the seat, I kept repeating what Wahaya said so I could ask Bidziil what it meant. Once I was seated, Shana took off, and we were going faster than I knew a UTV could go.

When we arrived back at the lodge and were inside, I looked at Shana, "Why were you flying? He wasn't going to hurt us. He even said something like 'Wado, a-ya weh-ya.' Whatever that means. I think it was a thank you, maybe. I don't know, but it seemed to resonate as a thank you."

Bidziil overheard me and said, "He spoke to you again and called you, his beloved. Ursula, may I use your landline, please?"

Aunt Ulla went with Bidziil into the lodge office to use the phone. Shana, Mark, Adohi, and I all looked at each other. Adohi shrugged and went back to his laptop and started gaming again. I motioned for Mark, Shana, and I to move into the kitchen.

Mark looked at Shana quizzically, "So, did you see him or hear anything?"

Shana shook her head, "No, I didn't hear or see anything. I did feel like there was something there. But I didn't sense any danger, surprisingly."

As we walked into the kitchen, I added, "Mark, when he spoke, it wasn't out loud, it was in my mind, and he didn't move out of the forest. He stayed at a safe distance. Now, not to change the subject—but, yes, let's change it. Since it seems I've pretty much slept the day away—well, except for our little excursion to the lake—I think I'll take responsibility for making dinner. I know we have some leftovers, unless you guys got to them earlier or Aunt Ulla put them in with the food for our friend, Wahaya. But I think I'll make some homemade beef stew. Does that sound good?"

I looked up from the cookbook I had unconsciously grabbed and been browsing through to see Mark and Shana staring at me.

"What, would you rather have something else, or do you want to cook? Do I have something on my nose? Why are you two staring at me like that?"

Shana spoke up, "You didn't call it a creature or a dogman. You called him by the name Tsali suggested. You're giving him human qualities."

Looking at her, surprised, I then glanced down, sighing, "I guess I am. The more I think about it, what Tsali said, the lore, the emotions I've picked up on, and the fact that he talks. I think maybe I should, don't you? It's easier."

Right then, Aunt Ulla and Bidziil joined us in the kitchen. Bidziil took a deep breath before starting, "Ash, I just spoke with Tsali and let him know what the dogman said, and that your Wahaya's been watching the lodge—or more likely, you. I noticed a large shadow near the forest line last night before I left. Tsali consulted the Elders while we were on the phone. He shared what you told him yesterday, and then again today. They are not sure, but they suspect that either you are, or he thinks you are, his beloved who died. The Elders think you need to know the full story of Wahaya and his bride, especially since the dogman is watching you. Tsali wants you to know the story now rather than wait until he can get here tomorrow. Come... sit by me and I will tell you what was learned."

He patted the stool on the other side of the kitchen counter next to him. I sat down, while still holding the cookbook, as if it were my lifeline or something.

Bidzill cleared his throat and began the story, "Supposedly, Wahaya was the first in line to be Chief of the main tribe on the mountain and of the Guardian Night Warriors. He was to marry the daughter of another Mountain Tribe Chief. They had grown up together, knowing each other's thoughts and actions since birth. If she hurt herself, he would immediately know and run to comfort her. A shaman once told her father that they had been in love even when they were stars in the sky. The Chief's daughter, Ahyoka, and Wahaya were married in a special ceremony—not only binding them together as man and wife but binding their souls for eternity. They chose that ceremony because they felt and moved as one.

"Everyone knew they were destined to be together and knew of no deeper love. Except for one woman in a neighboring tribe who had always been jealous of Ahyoka. The wedding ceremony was joyous, and their night of passion was explosive. A union not only in bodies and souls, but one that also brought all the mountain tribes together in unity. Wahaya would be Chief and a well-respected leader one day, and was to stay in his human form, but had the ability to communicate and guide the dogmen of the night. Anyway, the morning after their wedding night, while Wahaya was meeting with his father-in-law and the Elders of all four tribes, the jealous woman snuck into the newlywed's hut and killed Ahyoka while she slept in their wedding bed. The woman was mad and thought that if she took Ahyoka's heart, she would then belong with Wahaya. When she was caught, she was wearing Ahyoka's wedding dress that was covered in her blood and was holding Ahyoka's heart. Wahaya went mad, wanted to take revenge on the woman, but the tribe held him back because it was the mother of Ahyoka, and the women who would choose the punishment, not the husband or men of the tribes.

"Ahyoka's mother was distraught and, in her mad state, while the women of the tribes encircled the two - she stabbed the crazy woman to death. Releasing her pain and anger only to become a shell of herself. The Chief could not officially mourn his daughter because he had to show strength, hold his tribe and now his wife together as best as possible. All the members of the tribe were shattered over the murder, and they knew what might come from this betrayal. You see, the crazy woman was Ahyoka's cousin and from a sister tribe. The Chief had to be careful how things were handled, and that is why Ahyoka's mother was the one to inflict the punishment. No one would question the love of a mother. That was when Wahaya chose to take on the dogman form, becoming the first of the Guardian Night Warriors to do so. He was set to be the Chief, but he became the first dogman instead. He was made of unimaginable strength, sharp cunning, heightened senses, and the deepest pain anyone could know. A loss like no other that would drive him forward to protect the mountain and its people. So, when he caught your scent, he also picked up on the essence of your soul that was once Ahyoka... and now is within you."

As I listened to Bidziil tell the story of Ahyoka and Wahaya, my heart ached for them, for her mother, her father, both of their families, and all the tribes. Tears welled up, and there was a heaviness of pain in my chest. I was grateful to Tsali for getting permission to share Wahaya's story with me, and then to Bidziil for telling me. Now that I had a better understanding, I would try to keep that in mind when dealing with Wahaya.

Bidziil went on to say, "Tsali and the dogman have formed a respect for one another. Wahaya asked that you be told the full story. Oh, and when Tsali spoke to the Elders, they asked if you would be willing to meet with them, at least on a video chat of some kind, since you're sort of stuck here. They have questions regarding Wahaya and the surroundings in your dreamtime."

Trying not to laugh at the visual of Elders sitting around a table, passing a pipe, and using computer video chat, I said, "Sure, I can meet anytime and, frankly, the sooner the better. I'm glad Tsali will be here. I just hope the snow doesn't give him too much trouble. I'm not going to ask how he's getting up here in the snow—I figure he's one of the Elders who has a modified truck, like you. But it'll be nice to have another elder here, to help you fend off my questions. So, all I want to know is what everyone wants for dinner? I'm hungry."

Bidziil chuckled as he agreed that having Tasli at the lodge would be good.

I looked down at the cookbook, then back up to see everyone looking at me like I had just sprouted antlers, so I asked, "What? Why are you looking at me so weirdly?"

Aunt Ulla spoke up first while the others nodded their heads in agreement, "No, dear. It's just that—are you okay? You're acting as if this is a regular day and there isn't a huge wolf-like man out there that seems to have you in his sights."

I sighed, "I'm fine and not as freaked out as I was at first—I'm not dismissing anything, but until Tsali is here, there really isn't anything more to talk about. Once he's here, then we'll hopefully find out if there is more to this pull towards each other than him thinking I might have something to do with his deceased bride. If I need to be concerned, I will be. But right now, I don't want to—I want to just be, without worrying over anything. Even a huge, scary creature that could kill me just as quickly as he could lick his paw. I get it, but right now I'm not going to focus on anything outside. I'm going to fix us dinner, and since no one spoke up as to what they wanted, I'm fixing beef stew. Now, go and do something other than stare at me. I love you guys, and I appreciate your care and concern, but let's have at least one night of normal, please."

With that, the men shrugged and went into the lounge, where I could hear them discussing what to watch. Thank goodness Aunt Ulla had the foresight to make sure there was satellite, Wi-Fi, internet—all the stuff to help keep bored people, especially men, content. Hopefully, it'll hold up at least through most of the storm. So far, so good, but if not, there are board games and a well-stocked library.

The three of us ladies decided to save the beef stew for later and changed the menu to burgers, corn on the cob, homemade mac-n-cheese, and baked potatoes. I also prepped tomorrow's meal, so all I had to do in the morning was take it out of the fridge and put it in a crockpot. Eight hours of slow cooking should make the roast nice and tender.

Once we finished cooking dinner and everyone was seated at the table, I felt a warmth running through me. Without thinking, I said out loud, "He likes it."

Conversations stopped, and all eyes flew to me. Realizing I spoke out loud, I shrugged, "Sorry, I felt... that he... liked the stuff we left." Then I quickly took a big bite of my burger to make sure I couldn't say anything else for at least a few moments.

Bidziil somberly looked at me, then my aunt, before saying, "The link seems to be growing stronger, faster than I would have thought."

They both sighed, and Shana sensed that I did not want to talk about it, so she spoke up, "Ash, what did you put in these burgers? They're the best I've ever had! Have you thought about opening a restaurant or food truck? I forgot how awesome your cooking is."

Mark and Adohi both hummed in agreement with a mouthful of their burgers.

"Never really considered it," I answered, swallowing hard. "I love to cook, but I enjoy cooking for my family and friends. I wouldn't want to make it a job, might not like it as much if I did."

With that, everyone seemed to focus on their food with very little talking except asking someone to pass something. Eventually, everyone was done eating and was rubbing their stomachs, saying how full they were, and they were glad there wasn't dessert tonight because they didn't want to ruin the taste of the burgers.

Everyone helped take the dishes into the kitchen and then Mark and Bidziil announced they were tired and went to get ready for bed. Adohi went to his room too, probably to game, which left Shana, Aunt Ulla, and me to clean up. Aunt Ulla was yawning, so I suggested that she go on to bed and that Shana and I could take care of things. Surprisingly, Aunt Ulla agreed. She gave me a hug and thanked both Shana and I, then she quickly left the kitchen.

"Did she just skip out of the kitchen, or was I seeing things?" I asked Shana with a chuckle as I started putting the dishes in the dishwasher.

"No, you saw her skip out. I don't think she was headed to her room either," Shana answered, laughing between us laughing.

We quickly fell into a cadence and had the kitchen spotless, ready to start all over tomorrow. I made both of us a steaming hot toddy to take with us to our rooms.

"I think I'm ready to head up too. I might do a little work, but after I drink this, I'm pretty sure I'll be knocked out," I told Shana as we grabbed our cups and headed out of the kitchen.

"Why did you make yours so hot? It has steam coming off it." She said, blowing on hers before trying to take a sip.

"I made mine hotter because I plan on taking a nice, long bath in that amazingly large garden tub. I can sip on my toddy while the tub fills, and I'll turn the jets on to allow myself to float away into calm. Before you say anything, I promise to stay aware so that I don't fall asleep and drown. I just want to relax, read a book, and turn into a prune. It's been a while since I've done that."

We made it to the top of the stairs, and I gave one final look over my shoulder to make sure we turned out all the lights. I remembered that Shana made sure all the doors were locked before we made our drinks, so all is good there. There was a solemn type of peace in the lodge with all the lights out, the embers slowly burned out in the huge Inglenook fireplace, and a quiet hum from the outside lights and the appliances rang through the place. I turned to Shana, smiled, and added, "The toddy will probably knock you out pretty quickly, so sweet dreams."

As I grabbed my doorknob, she said, in a barely audible tone, "You too, Ash, and I hope you get some answers tonight."

I walked into my suite and noticed my balcony door was slightly ajar, snow flurries were blowing in, and on my bed were several flowers. My favorite flower, nonetheless, is Hellebores— better known as Lenten Roses. A beautiful, deep purple color, the flower symbolized rebirth, resilience, and hope. I gently picked up the flowers, then looked around for something to put them in. My water bottle would have to serve as a vase until tomorrow.

Then, as I went over to shut the balcony door, I noticed the large footprints in the snow that showed something had come over the railing both ways. I looked out towards the forest line and saw a dark figure with two scarlet eyes. Without thinking, I halfheartedly waved and, realizing what I had done, I walked back in and closed my balcony door, locking it too. I quickly closed the curtains, stripped down, and headed to the tub. I downed my no-longer-hot toddy before stepping into the warm water.

Chapter 6

I was back in the center of the forest clearing, except this time the ground was covered in snow with a light dust falling still. The only light to see by came from a sliver of the moon. As I tried to look around, my senses went on high alert. Stepping out from behind a tree was the creature... Wahaya step he took towards me shook the ground, and I could feel the heat coming off his silky-smooth fur.

I admired how muscularly beautiful he was, and a shiver ran down my back, though I wasn't sure if it was fear or something else. I tried to speak, but the closer he got, words refused to come. So, I allowed my eyes to speak for me.

My gaze was drawn to his footsteps, then travelled up his massive calves that tensed with power as each foot landed. My gaze moved to his thighs, which were corded muscles that flexed as he slowly moved closer, allowing me to take in every inch of him. Another shiver ran through me. My eyes continued up, and I paused to catch my breath. By the time I made it to his broad chest, I was in pure awe of this God-like being.

He looked down at me and was so close I could feel the heat of his breath on the top of my head. I wasn't short by any means, but my 5'5" height was nothing compared to his, at least, 7 feet.

I slowly looked up and met his flaming amber eyes, as a slow, wicked smile crept its way onto his face. He took one final step closer, and the heat radiating off his body could have melted the snow if this wasn't a dream. He raised his hand, slowly, as he did previously, but this time he paused for a moment—as if he was unsure, and then he tenderly touched my cheek, rubbing his finger along my jawbone, feeling my skin. Then, moving slowly, he caressed the curve of my neck, which sent hot tingles throughout my body. He left lingering goosebumps from his touch on my collarbone and shoulder. My body betrayed me, leaning into his touch.

Hesitantly, he began walking around me—following the path of his touch, running his hand down my side to my hips, then up my back, only stopping to lean in and deeply breathe in my scent. Which brought a deep moan from him that vibrated my core. His touch began to take on more of a caressing feel. As he walked in front of me, he was no longer the creature I saw, but a God of absolute beauty.

He had transformed into one of the most gorgeous men I had ever seen. He appeared to be of Native American descent with high cheekbones and long, silky, obsidian black hair. And his once scarlet eyes were now coal black with a hint of a flame in them.

I couldn't help myself. I reached out hesitantly and touched his bare chest, looking into his eyes of dark pools where I swam in his gaze. We stepped even closer to each other, entranced, and spiraled into each other's souls. His lips lowered to meet mine, and it was as if we became one, heart to heart. Our kiss grew deeper and more desperate until I felt like I would lose my breath.

Reluctantly, we pulled apart. With our foreheads pressed together, he spoke to me in his sultry, deep voice, " Tsigaso Ꮎa. Ꮳhb ᎠhᎬh ᎠhᏴᏃᎩꮁ ꭱᏁᏴꞓhᏝᏴꞓꭱ hꮧᏒᎩ ᏴᎾ ꮪᏃꞓ40ᏬᎩ ꮿꞓꭰᎩ Ꭰ4ᏁᏬᎤ4ᏝᏍᎾꭰᎩꭰᏔꭰᎩ. ᏔhᎩᎠᏍᏣᎫᎫ ꮬhꮬ ᏴᎾ Ꮳhb ᏁꭲᏍᎢꮁ ꮪhᏁᎫꮻᏁᏴꭰᎤᎤ. ᏍᏏꭳᏝᏁᎾꭰᏓ ᏔhᏴᎾ hᏉᎢꮧᎩ ᎢᎾᏝᏣᏔᏍꭳ ᏴᎾ Ꮳhb."

I looked into his dark, sad eyes and whispered, "Your words are beautiful, but I don't understand what you're saying."

Realization crossed his face as he smiled and murmured, "Ah, yes, Tsali said you do not speak the old language." He drew in a deep breath, his voice low and reverent as he breathed, "My love... My Ahyoka reborn, you have returned to me. I am yours, and you are mine, through death and time. We are bound to one another for eternity."

At that moment, it was as if some ancient bond snapped into place, and a deep, resonating knowing filled my soul as I gazed into his eyes.

Then my brain decided to ruin the moment, I stepped back from him and folded my arms in front of me. I shook my head and said, "Wait, you aren't interested in me then. You only see your lost love. I might be your Ahyoka reborn, but right now, in this time, I'm me... and I have questions. Plus, I don't understand what's going on between us. Things are moving fast, and I need some time to process. No matter how gorgeous and, and.... breathtaking you may be. I just have to understand more."

As I turned away, I could feel him come up behind me and put his hands on my shoulders so he could pull me into his chest. I felt his hands begin to change again into those of the dogman as he placed a kiss on the side of my head, and he said, "I will do whatever it takes for you to know me again. Tsigaso Ꮎa, just please try. Give me—"

And then there was no sound.

I turned around to say something, only to see Wahaya, the forest, and the snow fading into darkness.

~

For a moment, I was afraid of the emptiness, then I heard knocking on my bedroom door. Relief swept through me. I was home in my bed, not in the middle of the forest.

Then I heard Aunt Ulla, "Ash, honey, are you okay? You slept through breakfast. Shana said to let you sleep and that you needed it, but I had to come check on you. I saved you a plate."

Almost yelling so she could hear me through the door, I shouted, "Thanks, Aunt Ulla, I'll be down in a few. Hey, could you have Shana come up?"

"Sure, dear, I'll send her up and see you downstairs when you two are done with girl talk." I heard her laughing through the door, then there was silence.

I smiled to myself because this moment reminded me of a time when Shana and I stayed here once during college. But not wanting to miss out on anything downstairs, I hurried out of bed, ran to the bathroom, and started getting ready.

Shana knocked on the door as she entered, "Ash? Your aunt said you needed me."

I poked my head out of the bathroom and started rattling off to her about the flowers. "Do you see the Lenten roses on my nightstand?"

"Yeah, where did you get them? They're beautiful. Aren't they further up the mountain and deeper in the forest? Please, tell me you did not go out last night and get them."

Stepping out of the bathroom, I replied, "No, no, I'm not that silly. No, when I came in here last night, my patio door was slightly open, and the flowers were on my bed. Also, he came to me in a dream."

"What?! Really? Tell me what happened! Did he say anything?"

I could feel a blush warming my cheeks as I told her about the dream, down to the steamiest detail. I fanned myself as I told her about the kiss—even remembering it sent tingles through me. I paused too long as I remembered the consuming darkness and how he faded out mid-sentence.

"Ash, what's wrong?" Shana asked, "You just stopped talking and got a strange look on your face."

"Sorry, I was thinking about how everything faded out. I mean, he was in the middle of saying something. It was almost like he didn't have control or was being pulled from the dream. It felt weird and void of energy. It was terrible. I had just told him that it didn't matter if I was his reincarnated love or not, I'm me now, and he had started saying something about doing whatever it takes, and then he was gone. There was something odd about the way he disappeared. I hope Tsali will shed some light on all of this."

Shana heard my stomach growl and suggested that we hurry downstairs to eat before everyone thought the dogman got in the house. We both laughed as I pulled on my shoes, then we headed downstairs.

Before we reached the last step, I stopped Shana, "Please don't tell anyone about any of it, okay? I'll tell them when the time is right and, I think, I want to talk with Tsali about this first."

"Yeah, I get it. He might be able to explain a few things— especially the fade out. Oh, and I do have to say... your Wahaya, he brought you your favorite flower, which had to mean something. I think that was really sweet, especially for whatever he is."

I stood at the bottom of the stairs and glanced out the window towards the back of the lodge. I noticed something towards the end of the deck area. It was the tote that had the food in it, and he'd set another flower on top of the tote. Shana noticed where I was staring and turned to look, then she gasped.

"Oh my God, he brought it back and with flowers." She looked back at me, she said, "I think you're going to have to tell everyone about last night."

"I know, but let's wait until Tsali gets here, that way I don't have to repeat everything several times. Okay?"

"Okay, why don't you go get your flowers and tote, and I'll distract the others until you come back in. But hurry, I'm only so good at diversion tactics."

Shana then headed for the kitchen, and I quietly went out back to hide the tote and the flower.

I met Aunt Ulla in the kitchen, where she outdid herself with the huge plate she saved me. Since everyone else had already eaten, I decided to eat at the counter. Breakfast was filling and yummy—homemade biscuits and gravy with a side of hash browns, eggs over easy, honey and jam on the side, bacon and sausage, along with strong coffee and orange juice.

By the time I was finished, I felt like I was waddling. But the food was so good. Now that I was satisfied and full, I joined the group who, apparently, were still full as well and joked about napping. Luckily, it seemed none of the others noticed the tote and flower that Wahaya left. I smiled to myself, remembering my dream and the flowers.

Before anyone could head to take said nap, there was a knock on the door. Mark, being the unofficial protector of the group, went and answered it. He came back in with Tsali and two other gentlemen. I noticed Aunt Ulla stiffen when she saw the taller man walk in. Tsali introduced the other Native man as Dusti Adeloquasti, then said the taller man was Mr. R. J.

Skullthorn, the owner of Dead Hollow mining company, and that he pulled up as they were getting out of the truck.

Aunt Ulla came forward and spoke up before Mr. Skullthorn had time to say anything, "Mr. Skullthorn, if you are here to try and get me to sell again, you might as well leave. I am not now, or ever, going to sell YOU my property. And once I'm gone, it will go to my niece, and she will never sell either—especially to you. So, why are you here?"

Not skipping a beat, Mr. Skullthorn smiled, slimily, and said, "Ursula, you wound me. I'm just here to check on you. The storms have been bad and are supposed to get worse. I just wanted to make sure you were okay and see if you needed anything. I feel I have a duty to help those who are fragile or of an elderly age."

I thought my aunt was going to pole vault over the sofa and strangle him by the look on her face, but nope, she held it together.

Aunt Ulla seethed, "Mr. Skullthorn, as you can see, I am perfectly fine, and I'm not alone. I have friends, family, and loved ones here to help me and get anything I may need. You may not know, but I have been on the mountain for over twenty-five years. I helped my late husband build this lodge. I am EXTREMELY capable of taking care of myself. Now, if you don't mind, please leave. I would like to spend time with my family and friends."

She started walking to the front door, heavily suggesting that he get out.

As he opened the door to leave, he turned and looked at all of us before saying, "You and your family might want to be careful, Ursula. There is something out in the woods, and it just might not like you being here anymore. Who knows— there may be more than one. You might want to make sure you all stay inside, and let's hope you have plenty of firepower. Oh, and you may want to keep your lights on. Have a good day, Ursula."

No one said anything or moved until he shut the door. Then Mark went to the window and watched as he drove away. Once he had pulled out of the driveway, Mark turned and huffed out, "He's gone, the bastard. The audacity of him to waltz in here and insinuate that Aunt Ulla is feeble and old. What an ass!"

Aunt Ulla, still seething, snapped, "Fragile, not feeble. But I'm neither, the rat."

Remembering the rat's introduction, I had to ask, "So, what does the R.J. stand for?"

Bidziil had moved to calm my aunt and took a moment to answer me, "His full name is Richard Jackson Skullthorn, but he likes to go by RJ."

Being the more sarcastic one of the group, I asked, "So, are all Richards... dicks? What the hell was that about?"

Aunt Ulla sighed before she filled me in, "Mr. Skullthorn owns a company that has been drilling on the mountain. Those living on the mountain were able to get an injunction, and he was forced to stop. The only way he could start up again, which will destroy the mountain, is if I sell. Since we own the largest portion of property, it wouldn't do him any good to buy everyone else out. Even if he bought the surrounding areas, he would still need this one to complete the project and make his investors happy. The lodge sits in the heart of the mountain, and he desperately needs it. But if he were able to get his hands on this place, everyone else would pretty much have to sell, and he knows that. He's tried several times, with each offer getting larger. I'd never tell him—but the last amount he offered was almost tempting. When I turned him down, he moved into using bullying tactics. Then Bidziil caught him near the back gate, where someone had busted a huge hole. He apologized and blamed it on one of his workers for being drunk. Then there were a few other things that were caught and fixed quickly. We hadn't heard anything from him in weeks - until today. I hoped we got lucky, and he was eaten by your dogman, but, apparently, that was not the case."

Adohi spoke up then, "Excuse me, but what did he mean when he said there was something in the woods and that it might not like us being here? And that you might need some firepower and to keep the lights on. That was weird, don't you guys think so?"

Now that the angry energy had left the room, we all sat down again, inviting Tsali and Dusti to join us. Aunt Ulla asked if she could get anyone anything to drink or snacks, but we were still coming down from Mr. Skullthorn's visit and full from breakfast.

I looked around and, since no one seemed like they wanted any food, I answered, "Thanks, Aunt Ulla, but I think we're okay for now. Why don't you relax a little? And, yes, Adohi, I think it was a threat. Sounded like he knows about Wahaya, too, or the others." I sat down on the arm of a big chair next to Shana.

Everyone nodded their heads in agreement. Adohi looked a little puzzled, but no one chose to enlighten him on what was happening. From what Bidziil had said earlier, Adohi wasn't in touch with his mountain roots. One of the reasons he was brought here but he thought it was a rogue bear with mange. They're scary, and deadly too.

Tsali spoke up and asked me to step away with him for a moment. Everyone watched with curiosity as we got up. We headed out to the back patio, and I grabbed my coat while slipping out the door first. Apparently, I had a new habit of checking for Wahaya on the other side of the lake, hidden amongst the trees. I sighed when I didn't see or sense him, and Tsali must have noticed.

"You look for him?" Tsali asked as he caught me looking to the lake and then to the cooler, which was set off to the side with the Lenten rose still on it.

Smiling at Tsali, I nodded, "Yes, yesterday we took some blankets and food out for him. I spoke into the woods and hoped he would hear me. I let him know that if he liked the food and wanted more to bring the chest back, and I would fill it with more food. We have plenty and giving him, some may keep him from killing... deer, a pet, or a person—if that is something he might do."

Tsali was staring across the lake as he quietly spoke, "Miss Ashley, the Elders believe that you are connected to him through the past life you heard of last night. Bidziil said that he told you of the legend of Wahaya's wife, Ayhoka, and the events that happened... her death.

"Yes, he did, and it was horrible. I hate that that happened to them, but as I said to Wahaya—I don't care if he thinks I am his dead wife, reincarnated or not. I'm me now, and the current me is what matters."

"You... you spoke to him? When, how? Bidziil did not tell me that you have seen him again. Did he try to attack you or—"

"No," I cut him off, "no. He came to me in another dream last night. In this dream, he first came to me as the dogman but then turned into his human form. He disappeared mid-sentence, too. It was strange. But you should also know that he brought me flowers—last night, before the dream, and another one on top of the cooler this morning." Under my breath, I muttered, "My favorite flower too."

"Miss Ashley, you said he disappeared... Was it a slow fade, or rapid, or how? It could give us a clue as to what is going on. The Elders and I feel that the evil that is happening on the mountain has grown stronger in the last day or so. We want to do our best to stop it, so we need as much information as possible."

"Well, when he disappeared, it was a quick fade, and I felt that he didn't want to leave, but maybe he was being pulled out by something or someone? He had a pained look on his face. Tsali, I'm concerned. Please don't think I'm crazy. I know I said earlier that I didn't want to see him, or have him come to me in my dreams, or, honestly, have anything to do with a freaking dogman, connection or not. Honestly, I'm torn on how fast this thing between us is moving—it's extremely scary. Other than a few hook-ups here and there when I was younger, I've never had a relationship move this fast. Not that this is a relationship, it's not. But... Tsali, I can't stop thinking about him, and each hour it seems like the connection gets stronger. I was wrong to try to deny whatever this is. Not that anything will or can happen. I mean—he is a dogman, after all, so physically nothing could ever happen... well, unless he can turn into a human man and then we..." I trailed off and cleared my throat.

"Anyway, Tsali, what I'm saying—in a roundabout way—is that I agree with you and the Elders on pretty much everything. I think something... I'm not sure how to say it, but maybe predestined stuff is going on. If I didn't think so before, I do now. And after our visit from Mr. Skullthorn. There was a heavy strangeness to his visit, almost like he wanted something to be wrong, and then what he said to Aunt Ulla, that was just rude. On top of it, what he said when he was leaving tells me that he knows about Wahaya or the other dogmen. Hell, he could be behind all this. I didn't like him when he walked in, and I really didn't like him after what Aunt Ulla told us. So, what I'm rambling on about is if I can help in any way, I will, just let me know what I can do."

"Could you call out to Wahaya and ask him some questions that might help?" He asked, "I will give you a few questions to ask him. The Elders have given me things to research, so I feel it is better for you to speak with him. If we can work together, maybe we can not only find out what or who woke Wahaya out of his peace but also stop the drilling."

"The drilling?" I thought I knew what he meant, but I needed clarification: "Are you talking about the mining?"

"Yes, the mining. Mr. Skullthorn is the owner of the largest mining company here. They have slowly been destroying a large section of the mountain. He says that they aren't stripping the land to get to the coal, but they are. The company spokesperson said they replant any trees that are destroyed, but they have yet to plant one tree in the years they have been mining. They are also encroaching on land that is not to be mined - sacred land. Several locals have caught them destroying and not replenishing anything. The area is suffering, and we must stop them. Your aunt has been a major voice against him and his company. What he said earlier, I would take it as a threat, and you all need to be wary and watchful. But as for Wahaya, since you are open to speaking with him, I would like to take you into a type of meditative state. I won't be with you in the meditation, but I will be able to bring you out immediately if needed. I can monitor you, and if there are any signs of distress, I will end the session. Would you be willing to do this? We would need to do it soon."

"Yes, I'll do it! When can we? Do you want to stay, and we could do it tonight, or do you have to prepare or—?"

Holding his hand up to slow me down, Tsali said, "Soon. I need to consult with the other Elders, but possibly late tomorrow. I brought Dusti, one of the other Elders, with me to meet and speak with you. I wanted him to be here with us to discuss Wahaya and the other dogmen. It is good to have as much information as we can, and Dusti has been around longer than all of us. He is a relative of Ahyoka, Wahaya's past wife. And since we know there are at least two other dogmen, he should be able to help with questions you may have about Ahyoka. Let's go in, and I will introduce you."

"Okay. Oh, and please don't tell anyone about my dreams or that he brought me flowers. I've only told Shana and you about this second dream; I'm not ready to tell the others yet."

He nodded his head and guided me in after we both stopped for a moment to look across the lake. I wasn't sure if he felt it or not, but we were being watched—except I didn't feel that it was Wahaya. There seemed to be a heavy sort of darkness, and it wasn't from Wahaya's usual location. This felt closer and not safe. I knew deep down it wasn't him.

Chapter 7

As I walked Tsali and Dusti out to Tsali's truck, we continued the conversation about Wahaya. Earlier, Dusti filled me in on a bit more of the dogman lore. Apparently, after the transformation ceremony was completed, there were a few other dogmen who wanted his title. They challenged him, and even together they still lost the fight, and left the pack to wander. There were two that worked together and tried to kill Wahaya, but they failed. It is thought that one of them was one of his closest friends until they became dogmen. According to Dusti, something happened to them during the ritual that drastically altered a few of their personalities. Dusti also ensured that there were many Elders working around the clock on this, including him, Bidziil, and Tsali.

I thanked them for coming by, saying that it was a pleasure talking to Dusti and learning more about the dogman lore, and that I would keep Tsali updated on any happenings around the lodge and my dreams.

Suddenly, Dusti stopped, he turned to the woods across from the lodge, and his color turned pale, almost like he'd seen a ghost.

"Miss Ashley, please go into the house at once," he said, quickly. "You all will want to pull the storm shutters down and keep them locked until this is all over. I will have Tsali call you later, but for now, please go in and lock everything up. Please stay inside for the rest of the night, possibly several days. But please go, now, *NOW!*"

Not wanting to stress him anymore, as he looked scared out of his wits, I turned and ran to the house, stopping only after I got the front door open and turned to watch them back up. Tsali waved as they peeled out of the driveway. I suddenly felt a heavy darkness and knew we were being watched by something evil.

As I shut the door, I heard, "Hey Ash, do you want to take some food to your friend? I saw that he brought the cooler back. Bet he's hungry again." Mark said as he came bouncing around the corner, only to stop dead in his tracks when he saw my face.

"No, not today. I need to speak with everyone, *now*, let's get them in here and hurry!" I said as I went rushing past him and started to lower the shutters.

Mark looked at me like I'd lost my mind, but saw the fear on my face and stuttered out, "Ahmm, sure I'll go get them. You okay?"

Rushing to the next window, I turned and looked at Mark, "I'm fine, just go, and I'll explain when everyone is here."

I wasn't sure if I understood exactly what Dusti was trying to tell me, but I picked up on his fear and then the heaviness. I'm not that empathic; he was just that scared. While I waited for everyone to come in, I kept lowering and locking the shutters around the main lodge windows.

All of a sudden, I heard a bloodcurdling scream coming from the back. I ran as fast as I could through the house and saw Mark and Bidziil drag Adohi in the back door. Shana shut and locked it behind them, and Aunt Ulla started taking care of Adohi. His leg was bleeding from what appeared to be a huge slash.

Bidziil looked up at me and barked out, "Looks like your dogman didn't like what you gave him. He attacked Adohi! We saw him, then we started running back to the lodge when he dove at us and grabbed Adohi's leg. Luckily, I had my .38 and shot him. He howled and ran away."

I shocked all of them with one quick statement, "It wasn't him! There are more of them, and they're here to scare us, or worse. Aunt Ulla and Shana, can you two take care of Adohi for a bit? I need Mark and Bidziil to help me lock this place up and make sure we are ready for whatever might happen. Oh, and let's make sure to lock the shutters in Adohi's room too. We need to make sure we're protected all the way around."

Mark and Bidziil moved Adohi to his room, then worked on closing the rest of the shutters and locking everything. Mark ran down to the cellar and made sure that all the doors and windows were locked tight there. Shana and Aunt Ulla went to work taking care of Adohi, and I was glad Shana had some medical knowledge. She would be able to clean his wounds, bandage them, and maybe even stitch or tape up the slashes. I grabbed the emergency kit for them and helped give him some pain medication and something to help him sleep.

Aunt Ulla made sure years ago that the lodge emergency kit was like a mini hospital stash after I fell out of a tree, and it took us over an hour to get to the hospital. We even took classes on emergency procedures, so those two should be able to handle Adohi pretty quickly.

With Adohi settled in his room, Shana joined us in double-checking everything. Aunt Ulla stayed with Adohi to make sure he fell asleep okay. Once we were done checking all the locks, we gathered in the front room, and Aunt Ulla walked in just in time for Tsali to call. I put him on speaker after telling him what happened to Adohi.

Everyone was beyond quiet, so we could hear every word Tsali had to share, "I am so sorry for not calling you sooner, but Dusti wanted to be sure he was correct in what he thought he saw and felt when we left before I called you."

Bidziil, somewhat upset, said, "Did he or you have any idea there were more than one of these things on the property while you were here? We could have used the notice!"

Tsali paused for a moment, then said, "I apologize, everyone. I really do. But we did not know for sure until we drove down the mountain. We lost service until we reached town. While talking to Miss Ashley, he thought he felt we were being watched then, as we pulled out of the lot, he caught a glimpse of two creatures hiding in the shadows of the forest. They were not as well hidden as they might have thought, or maybe they wanted to be seen. He feels these creatures were sent to scare you all off the mountain, and possibly worse if you do not leave, which they may have just given you an example of. Miss Ashley, I agree with your thoughts that Mr. Skullthorn may have something to do with this—what, exactly, we don't know. But we will be doing all that we can to find out what is going on. Until we know more, all of you need to please stay inside, stay safe, and have heavy firepower just in case. Now, Miss Asley, will you please take me off, speaker?"

Kind of stunned, I was slow to hit the button, "Oh yeah, sure." I took the phone off speaker and placed it to my ear, "Thank you for calling back, and please let Dusti know that we appreciate his help too."

"Miss Ashley, please beware that there is a chance that they might be able to use the dream ability as well. They could try to harm or kill you in your sleep. Please be extremely careful and make sure that everyone stays indoors. Also, I will try to get back to perform the guided dreamtime with you, but it will depend on whether Dusti needs my help or not here. Until then, I need you to call out to Wahaya—just from your balcony, it's too dangerous from the ground floor, and then again while in your dreamtime. Please speak with him about the others and what's happening. Try to find out whatever you can that may be going on. Then, after you speak with him, please let me know; it may help us to figure out who is behind this evil."

"Of course, I'll call you in the morning. I just hope he'll come since we weren't able to take the cooler back out to him."

"I do not think he visits you because he wants a cooler full of food or blankets. It is for you that he visits, and he even visited before he knew you were his beloved. He is attracted to you. Anyway, please call out to him; you will want to make sure he speaks with you. Remember, please let me know as quickly as possible. Stay safe and goodbye, Miss Ashley."

"Goodbye, Tsali!" I hung up, then turned to the group and reiterated that we were all to stay inside no matter what and be prepared for the worst.

It was a good thing that when the lodge was built, it was made to withstand a warzone. My dear uncle remembered all the stories from his childhood of the creatures that lived on the mountain, and he wanted to make sure nothing could ever get in. And then my aunt had lived in an actual warzone, so he wanted her to feel protected from any evils that may come this way... human or otherwise.

I snapped out of my quick memory and noticed everyone was looking at me, "Sorry, I was thinking about something. So, everything is locked down tight, right?"

Mark's law enforcement training kicked into professional mode as he said, "Everything is locked tight. Downstairs and up—we locked up your rooms too. So maybe just check things and grab some stuff to take downstairs before it gets dark. I'm going to go grab the rest of my guns and ammo from my Jeep's lockbox. Bidziil, can you cover me and keep a lookout?"

Both Bidziil and Mark went to get his guns while Shana and I watched from the window. Aunt Ulla did a quick check on Adohi and then went to the kitchen to make something. Mostly to keep herself busy. Things were so crazy that we missed lunch. Once the guys were back in, I locked up the shutters again. Mark had a small arsenal in his Jeep's lockbox, and apparently, Bidziil grabbed the rest of his too. I guess we were set with firepower.

"Okay, I'm going to run upstairs and check my rooms. If you need me, yell," I said as I ran up the stairs.

I opened my bedroom door and saw that the patio was somehow ajar. I sucked in a breath as a moment of fear flashed through me, then I saw the flowers on my bed. I looked around to make sure I was the only one in my room, then I ran over to lock the patio door and check the windows. I know Mark said they got my room, but I rechecked anyway. I quickly went to my office and studio, making sure everything was locked up still. I pulled down the storm shutters, went back into my room, and then went out onto the balcony. I looked around and tried to see if there were any more signs of Wahaya or the others. I didn't see anything, but there was a strange smell—worse than any skunk spray I'd ever smelled before.

It must have been one, or both, of the others nearby because I'd not smelled this type of smell before. It was putrid. Not even when I first ran into Wahaya killing the deer. But then again, I was too scared to notice any smells. Since I couldn't see them, I wasn't sure where they were, although I could feel multiple pairs of eyes watching me. I tried not to take a deep breath because the smell was still strong, but I closed my eyes and mentally called out to Wahaya, asking him to come to me in my dreams.

As I opened my eyes, I heard a howl from across the pond in the direction where Wahaya was before. I could feel that the howl was him letting me know he received my message. I turned to go in, quickly locking the doors and pulling the bar down, securing the storm shutters. I used to think all these shutters and bar locks were silly, but right now, I was grateful for them.

I was headed back downstairs when I heard Adohi scream out, and all of us ran to his room. He was just having a dream, but then I remembered what Tsali said about the others having the ability to use the dream state.

I immediately started trying to wake him up.

Everyone else thought I was crazy, but once he was awake, he told us about his dream. I figured it could have been a mental attack—which it was.

Concerned, I looked at Bidziil and asked, "Bidziil, do you know of any way to protect us during our dreams? Apparently, these other dogmen can also move in dreams. If you don't, please call Tsali or one of the other Elders and find a way or we're going to have to take turns sleeping. And changing our sleeping habits won't be fun... at all."

Bidziil shook his head and said he didn't know of this, then ran into another room and started making phone calls. Aunt Ulla said she would stay with Adohi for a while if I took over in the kitchen and possibly started making dinner. Shana suggested moving him to the couch so he could play games, and that they might help keep him awake. After we had him settled, I went to the kitchen to see what Aunt Ulla had been working on. And apparently, she decided to make dinner early, but had only gotten the ingredients out.

Once dinner was ready and I had made up a tray for Adohi and Aunt Ulla, the others came in, got their food, and then joined Adohi and Aunt Ulla on the couch. Everyone got settled and started eating while Bidziil filled us in on what he had found out from the calls he made. The Elders gave him some ideas—suggesting that we take turns sleeping and we all sleep in the same area. The cellar would be the safest; we just had to get Adohi down there and set up some cots or inflatable beds - thankfully, the downstairs was as huge as the lodge. With an open area that has a huge fireplace, a fluffy couch, a few lounges, a large screen TV, and several rooms off on both sides, and a basement door that goes outside. Mark and Bidziil said they would stay upstairs and team up sleeping.

After finishing dinner, we worked to make the basement even more comfortable. Since the basement had at one time been a party and dance area, it was easy to make it a big comfy hideaway, and with the big screen, a game room for Adohi. Between those, we only needed two additional air mattresses. We filled the downstairs refrigerator with some food and restocked it with more drinks. Technically, we had a nice panic apartment.

We left the internal basement door open so the guys could run in if they needed to, or we could yell at them to wake up. By late evening, we were all set for the night. But now no one was sleepy. I told Shana that I was supposed to call on Wahaya, but I didn't feel like I could do it down here, knowing others were in the room. I decided to go back to my room, and I felt for some reason I knew he wouldn't let the others into our dreamtime, but I told her to check on me in a few hours.

Shana was skeptical and tried to talk me out of it, but eventually agreed as long as I left my room door open and kept one of the walkies near my bed. That way, she and Mark could hear if I was in distress. I agreed and grabbed one of the voice-activated walkies, so it was kind of continuously on.

Apparently, Aunt Ulla had purchased several so guests could call from their rooms if they needed anything. As usual, Aunt Ulla had found a simple, fun way to make her guests comfortable, which was such a good idea. I smiled at the thought as I headed upstairs.

I checked in with Mark and Bidziil, letting them know what I was doing. They weren't thrilled, but I explained that even though I knew how dangerous it was to be so far away from everyone right now, I felt that I would be safe. I knew deep down that Wahaya would protect me. Neither of them was thrilled, but they let me go upstairs again with the agreement that I would leave my door open and that if they heard the slightest sound, they would come up.

I gave them both a hug and went upstairs.

Once there, I checked my office and studio locks again and then headed to my bedroom. I checked to make sure that everything was still locked up, then I quickly took a hot shower, got ready for bed, and stood at the patio door looking out to the woods across the pond. Mentally, I called out to Wahaya, the man and the creature. As I turned to go in, I heard a familiar howl. I smiled to myself, then lay in bed, and as I closed my eyes, I took a few deep breaths and began mentally calling. I wasn't sure how long it was before the tiredness overtook me, but into the darkness I fell.

~

I found myself standing on the other side of the pond facing the woods. Wahaya was in his creature form as he came walking out from the trees. But the closer he got—he slowly shifted into a man.

Not thinking clearly, I ran to him, "Wahaya, there are more of you, except they are not like you, one of them attacked

98

Adohi. Do you know where they came from? Why are they here? Or, how you were all awoken, anything?"

He smiled down at me and put a finger to my lips, "Shh, we are not alone. They are watching but they cannot hear from where they are if we whisper. I'm going to pull you close and kiss you. If we kiss, they will think you are mine and hopefully leave you alone."

I looked into his eyes, and I could tell he wasn't messing with me. So, as he pulled me closer, I put my arms around his neck and—I wasn't sure what overtook me—but as he leaned in to kiss me, I met his lips and kissed him with a passion I'd never felt before. The kiss was warm, stirring something deep inside me and melting any coldness I may have felt in the beginning. He continued kissing me— my lips, my cheek, then around to my ear, where he began whispering answers to all the questions I asked while he continued to kiss me in between words.

"I'm sorry they attacked your friend. I hope he wasn't badly hurt. I do not know how we were awakened, or by whom, only that I awoke in my cave feeling angry and hungry. The others probably did as well. I can try to find out as much as possible and let you know."

I pulled him even closer as I whispered in his ear, "Since they're here, are they able to come to me in dreams too? I know one tried to hurt our friend. He said he was attacked in his dream, but we were able to wake him before anything happened."

As Wahaya continued his trail of kisses, he came to my other ear and told me, "They cannot come directly to you. They may follow me here, but that is because we were from the same tribe at one time. Only I have a connection with you, so I am the one who can come to you. The one that attacked your friend tasted his blood, which is why he can attack him in his dreams. Keep your friend up at night and let him sleep during the day with someone in the room. The others will keep their distance from us, especially if they think we are mated."

"Mated—but how could that happen if you're... a dogman?"

He softly kissed me, moaning against my lips, "We can be together in dream form, which to them will appear that we are mated. Dreams will have to sustain us until the day I am able to..."

Before he could finish what he was saying, there was a menacing howl that came from a not-so-far distance. He turned to see where it was coming from, then grabbed and kissed me passionately before backing away.

He mouthed "wake up, NOW," and he began to fade away.

As I watched him dissolve, I heard another loud howl growing closer.

~

I woke up, gasping, as I heard Mark calling my name and felt him shaking me.

I jumped up from my bed when I heard a loud bang on the side of the lodge. Mark shushed me and pointed at me to go downstairs. As I got up, I grabbed my sweater jacket and shoes, then ran out, closing the door to my room. Mark guided me out, and I followed him down to the basement, dressing as I went. On the way down, we heard growling outside the window and scratching on the side of the lodge. Mark and Bidziil stood their ground, with rifles ready.

I continued downstairs to let the others know what was going on and to call Tsali immediately—regardless of how late it was. When I reached the bottom of the steps, I saw that Adohi was starting to doze off, so I scared the crap out of him to wake him up. I told Shana, Aunt Ulla, and Adohi what Wahaya said and that staying awake at night would be the best way to keep them out of his dreams and sleep during the day with someone in the room. So of course, we'll keep a watch during the day, just in case.

After I gave them the report, I quickly tried to call Tsali. He must not have been asleep or slept lightly, because he answered on the first ring. I told him everything Wahaya said and that the other dogmen were there in the background of our dreamtime and were possibly attacking the lodge. When we hung up, he promised to go to the Elders immediately, and I promised to call him if anything happened or if I heard from Wahaya again.

Things seemed calm upstairs, so Shana went up to see if everything was clear. She yelled down and said that it was okay to come back up. Aunt Ulla had found some crutches for Adohi, so he was able to make it upstairs with minimal help. Once we were all upstairs, Bidziil suggested we come up with a sleep schedule.

Even though it had only been a few hours since we ate, I was a bit hungry. No one else wanted anything, so I went to the kitchen and made a quick snack. For some reason, I was drawn to look out the window. I slowly pulled back the curtain and peeked out into the semi-darkness. Staring back at me were a pair of sickly, golden-yellow eyes. I gasped and the creature snorted and smiled a wicked, snarling smile. It was a horrible, scary look, and it sent a chill down my spine. Then it backed up, turned, and ran off into the woods.

I staggered back from the shock, then ran into the living room where everyone could see the fear on my face. I took a deep breath to help gather my thoughts and told them what I had just seen and how the dogman acted.

"I think they only want to scare us right now. But it could change at any moment. I'm glad we're ready just in case," I said as I sat down, trying to steady my nerves.

Mark and Bidziil looked at each other, and then Mark said, "I'm going to call my old Marine buddy, Stephenson. We've been talking about him visiting for a hunt, and now might be the perfect time. Funny—I just spoke to him last week. He's moved into the area recently, so he should be ready. And he's not that far, so he can get up here within hours. He's one of the few people I know with a vehicle that can make it through this storm. He has an extensive military background and has dealt with some *strange* things before. If nothing else, he could take Adohi to the doctor and get you ladies out of here."

At that statement, Aunt Ulla stood up and went off, "I will *NOT* leave my home because of a few big dogs Skullthorn has sent to scare me off my land. If I leave, then Skullthorn wins, and I'll be damned if that's going to happen."

Jumping in on the idea, I said, "I'm not leaving either. I'll stay here with Aunt Ulla and help protect the lodge and make sure you don't kill the wrong creature."

Everyone looked at me like I was crazy.

"Yes, you heard me," I continued, "Wahaya isn't part of this scare tactic the other two are doing. I spoke to him, and he's going to help. He doesn't know how or why they were awakened, but he's going to try to find out. He has to be careful because they're watching him. At least one of them was in my dream, but stayed at a distance. He also said the reason one was able to attack Adohi in his sleep is that it was the one who attacked him. When it made physical contact and tasted his blood, a connection of sorts was created. Wahaya is able to communicate with me because there's a soul connection from our past life together. The rest of you should be able to sleep whenever, and I agree, it might be good if we do get Adohi out of here."

Surprisingly, Adohi looked up from his phone and said, "I'm not going anywhere. My leg is fine, and I've got crutches now. There's crazy stuff happening here, and I don't want to miss out. Plus, I'm supposed to learn from my granddad. I can't do that if I'm not here to participate and help. So, I'm not going anywhere, and... somebody has to keep me awake until this is over; nobody else is going to do that except you guys. So, I'm staying."

No one could disagree about keeping him awake, so we all accepted that he would stay. Mark was still concerned about Adohi's leg, so when he called his friend, he asked Stephenson to pick up more medical and surgical supplies as well as grab some penicillin. He then explained that Stephenson had also been a medic at one point, so he could help Shana with Adohi's leg and any other potential injuries.

I started to feel tired again. I guess all this excitement was getting to me, so I let everyone know that I was going to lie down for a few hours. I didn't feel like going upstairs, so I went to the library and curled up on the loveseat in the corner, leaving the door open in case I needed them. As I started to doze off, I called out to Wahaya, hoping that he could keep the others away.

Chapter 8

I was back in the forest, and Wahaya was standing in front of me, already in his human form. As he wrapped me up into a hug, he immediately shushed me with a kiss above my ear, "We are being watched. My love only speak in kisses and whispers."

He continued kissing my cheek and softly let me know that there was a man ordering the other two dogmen to get us out of the lodge and to then destroy it. They were told not to kill anyone—at least, not yet.

He also said he was able to hide where they couldn't see him, but he was able to hear most of what was being said—but that one of the others suspected him, so he wouldn't be able to visit as often.

"Ashley, I think it will be best for you and your friends to sleep during the day with one of you watching and then be awake at night. Your men may want to put up some type of wire around the lodge that could hurt our animal forms. I have seen such fences on other properties. It might only be a small deterrent, but it is still something."

He went on to say that the man ordering them to do all this was a white man, and that his shirt had a skull in a mountain hollow with smoke coming out of it. It was this man who found a way to wake them.

"I believe I was awoken by accident," he whispered, "It was my connection to you that allowed me to awaken with them. Luckily, they did not know I existed until recently. The other two have not let on that I am also awake. So, the man does not know."

Pulling back to look at him, I made sure to hide my fear because I could sense the others watching. Without thinking, I pulled him closer and kissed him. In a few short days, I'd gone from being scared to death of the creature he was to desiring the man he is and the one I am bound to.

The kiss grew deeper until I heard my name being called...

Dammit, Shana.

"I have to go. She's going to start shaking me to wake me up. I'll be back, and in the meantime, I'll see what information we can find. Be careful. I know you're a big, bad, dogman, but I'm kind of growing fond of you, especially your human form."

He kissed me, then whispered, "Be safe, my love. They may target you to get to me."

He began to drift into a fog, and then he was gone.

Then I realized he'd called me Ashley. Maybe that was his way of accepting me, as me.

~

Waking up perturbed, I shouted, "Damn it, this fading in and out shit has got to stop! Who is controlling that? Geez!"

Shana laughed, as she had just stepped into the room and brought in a tray with snacks.

"Did I miss a meal?" I asked, "I didn't think I slept that long. I thought my dream was short. It seemed like it started as soon as I closed my eyes and then ended a few minutes after." I looked at the cuckoo clock in the library, and I realized that it was approximately an hour since I'd first laid down.

"Shana, how has it been? Quiet... or, you know, not?"

Shana replied, "It's been quiet, thankfully. Mark is sleeping at the moment. I was able to get him to lay down right after you did. I'm not going to wake him up until he is absolutely needed or he wakes up on his own. Bidziil also went to sleep, so I'm glad it's been quiet. Now that we have daylight, I think we all should sleep while we can."

"Actually, since I just woke up from a short hour nap, I'll keep watch. I can sleep almost any time. Wahaya's been watching out for me in dreams, so I think I'm okay."

"I'll go sleep for a bit, I think," Shana said, "and let your aunt and Adohi know that you'll keep watch. Fingers crossed those things won't try anything. Maybe wake me up in about four hours? Unless something is going on and you need help, then wake one of the guys."

Shana chuckled as she got up and walked out of the library.

I sat up then hurried and ate some of what she brought, but I didn't really have an appetite. I ran back over the last few days and how I'd gone from getting rid of a deadbeat boyfriend to being involved with some legendary, God-like creature and having two other beasts come after us. Things have gotten weird really quickly, and I don't like the feeling of not being in control. Although when I truly look at things, having full control of anything is an illusion.

I stood up, stretched, and went to look out the window in the direction that the other two dogmen were originally seen, unsure what I was looking for, but thankful there was nothing there. It'd been nice having the quiet time to breathe and rest up, especially since it's usually quietest before the storm, they say. Not sure who said it, but it seems to be true most of the time. Hopefully not this time.

I decided to go get some dessert and make sure everyone else was sleeping, so I quietly crept out of the library. Still awake, my aunt sat on the couch eating a piece of apple pie, and on the table was another piece of pie and a cup of steamy coffee.

"Aunt Ulla, shouldn't you be asleep? And... Why do you have two pieces of pie and hot coco? Is Bidziil up too?"

"No, this isn't for Bidziil," she replied, "I heard you moving around and, knowing how you like your dessert almost immediately after a meal, I thought I'd have it ready for you. Everyone else is sleeping, so we can talk privately. I'm sure we all can agree that Jackson Skullthorn is behind this. He's an evil man, and I don't think he'll quit until someone—or all of us—are dead. Those creatures really are under his control, aren't they? I've been thinking... maybe I should sell the lodge to him. I don't want anyone else to get hurt, or worse, die, because I want to hold on to this place. He'll leave us alone then."

"No, Aunt Ulla, I don't think he will leave us alone." If you sell the lodge to him, he'll have to give up money. He's the type of person who would rather not pay out but would rather kill everyone, blaming it on some crazy animals, and get the land for free. He'll kill them, be the hero, and no one would be the wiser or, possibly, be too scared to challenge him. So, no, you cannot sell to him. If you want everyone to leave, I'll agree with that. But I'm not leaving. I know it's crazy, but Wahaya would protect me."

"Ashley, dear heart, are you sure? Just a few days ago, you wanted to get rid of the creature and had just broken up with your boyfriend. What's changed?"

I took a long drink of the coffee she had gotten for me, giving myself time to form my answer.

"I know, I'm not sure what to think either. Things have been weird these last few days. Richard and I were done a long time ago; I just stayed because, well, I was comfortable in my misery and didn't want to be alone. Plus, I was a bit lazy about leaving. It took seeing him with someone else to push me to do what I should have done a long time ago. It's not a good reason, I know, but that's it. As for our protective, furry friend, I can't explain it—but the connection has gotten stronger with each day and every time I see him, or think of him, it tightens. He kissed me, and it's like a fire has been ignited and is burning in my soul, my body. Every fiber of my being sparks to life with his touch, and there's a longing that lingers. I've never felt like this with anyone else, ever. He hasn't come to me in only his dogman warrior form since the first dream."

I had to adjust my position in the chair before I continued. As the heat began to build, I started talking about him.

"I've come to know him as Wahaya, the warrior, the man who brings me my favorite flowers. I didn't tell him what it was; he just knew. I didn't want to tell you, but he left Lenten Roses on my bed and then on the cooler when he returned them. He just knew. Aunt Ulla, this is kind of unusual for me to tell you, but I hope this helps explain what I feel. I come alive when he touches me; it's like he knows my body better than I do, and it's only a dream. I can't explain it, and what's just as strange is I don't want to. I just want to feel. I know it's probably not the right thing, and I mainly see the human part of him in dreams, but—"

Patting my hand, Aunt Ulla stopped me, "My dear, you don't have to explain it to me. Your uncle may not have been a sexy creature, but we connected quickly, too, and I had just dumped the guy I had been dating for two years at the time. He was a... what do you kids call it... a tool. Yes, he was a tool, somewhat like Richard. I dumped him and almost immediately met your uncle."

We both laughed a little, and then she continued, "Your uncle swooped in and caught me off guard. He was a gentleman—he never tried anything rash, and courted me with flowers, candy, and he showed me respect. He didn't care that I came from another country or that I couldn't give him children. Yes, he knew, and he still loved me. When he asked me to marry him, I didn't hesitate. I said yes so fast it would've made your head spin, and we were married three months after we met. There is no shame in what seems to be quick love if there is a real, deep connection. Who knows, maybe it had been there under the surface waiting to be found. And that's why you and Richard, or any others that you dated, never worked out. Strangely enough, I do believe you and this creature are connected. Whether you are his reincarnated wife or not doesn't matter; there is a connection, a soul-deep connection. Maybe the flowers are a sign."

"Thank you, Aunt Ulla. I'm grateful for your support. It means a lot to me. But right now, we just need to get through whatever this is. I wonder..." I couldn't figure out if I wanted to tell her my idea or not, so I chose not to finish what I started to say.

"Wonder what, sweetheart?"

"Never mind, I had an idea, but I need to check some things first before I speak it out loud." I hugged my aunt and, since the others were asleep, I didn't want to talk too loudly, so I whispered to her, "I'll get the dishes—you need to go get some sleep before the others wake up. I'll also get something started in the crockpot, so don't worry about what to fix for tomorrow or today. I'm confused on my days, apparently."

She thanked me, hugged me back, and then went to her room.

Once I was in the kitchen, I cleaned things up and put on a crockpot full of jambalaya. A recipe I learned how to make when I was visiting Shana during her time studying in the Bayou of Louisiana. While cutting up the ingredients, my mind wandered back to then and how I was surprised that she didn't see any paranormal creatures while there. I would have thought the Bayou would be full of strange things.

Maybe she did and didn't say anything because someone might've thought she was crazy? Could also be why she accepted Mark's view on strange things. And now Wahaya. Once everything calms down, I may just have to quiz her about her time in the Bayou. She might open up now if she did.

Lost in thought, I was startled by a loud knocking on the front door. I put everything down except the butcher knife I was holding. I slowly crept toward the door and peeked out the window. I was relieved when I saw that it was Tsali and another man, so I let out the breath I had been holding. I hurriedly opened the door, rushing them in and then locking the doors as quickly as possible.

"What are you doing here?" I asked, "It's not safe, and since the sun will be setting soon, you won't be able to leave until morning. If there is a morning for us."

Tsali took a step toward me, "Ms. Ashley, we are prepared to stay, and we have provisions in the truck. We need to get them quickly before the sun makes another move to set. Shall we?"

The three of us hurried to the truck and, after four trips, we were able to get everything in. They brought food, drinks, weapons, a lot of ammo, and quite a few ceremonial items.

While bringing things in, Tsali introduced his other friend as Elder Oukonunaka, or Okon, one of the greatest Elders and extremely knowledgeable about ceremonies, dogmen, and other creatures I had no desire to know of.

We chatted while putting things away, and, trying to keep the conversation light, we left the heavy talk for later. Once we were done and everything was in its place, we sat and talked over some strategies for dealing with any attacks or threats that might come up during the night.

The three of us made sure the items were organized for multiple rituals, since they planned on performing them in the basement once everyone was awake. They planned to raise a protection barrier around the lodge that would keep any cryptid or unnatural creatures out, thus giving them more time to hopefully lure the two evil dogmen under Skullthorn's control back to sleep. I wasn't sure if it was fortunate or unfortunate, but Wahaya might be included in the sleep.

We were quiet and started taking things to the basement. Okon took another trip back downstairs, bringing a few extra things, and on his way back up the steps, I stopped him to ask a question.

"Okon, umm, do you have to include Wahaya in the sleep ritual? I mean, is there a way to, I don't know, possibly turn him back into his human self?"

Okon looked at me with curiosity, but smiled and nodded, "Miss Ashley, I will consult with the spirits while we create the protective barrier. We will try to only keep the others away, but I cannot promise anything. There may be something we can do. Excuse me, we must get started if we are to have it up by nightfall."

He turned abruptly and went down the stairs.

Wow, a man of few words. Let's hope he says more to the spirits.

Chapter 9

The hum of chanting floated up from the basement, along with a strong smell of incense and sage. Bidziil and Mark came into the kitchen.

"What is that smell coming from the basement? Ash, can I have a cup of coffee, please?" Mark asked as he yawned.

"I know the smell and sounds well. The smell is of ceremonial herbs and sage. When did Tsali arrive? And which elder did he bring with him?" Bidziil added while getting a glass of water.

I chuckled as I saw Mark awkwardly stretching while he yawned, and Bidziil making a funny face imitating him.

"Good morning-ish to you two, too," I said, sarcastically, "Tsali introduced him as Okon, said it was easier than his real name. They got here about an hour ago, and they brought lots of supplies. Not only ceremonial things, but food, water, ammo, and a few extra weapons. It was a good thing everyone moved back upstairs to nap, because once they got the supplies downstairs, they immediately began arranging the ritual items for the ceremony. They got the first ritual started about fifteen minutes ago. It's to put up a protective barrier around the lodge, so it should prevent any more attacks. They also hope to be able to put the dogmen back in their slumbering state without killing them."

I heard my own voice and realized how sad I sounded.

Mark picked up on my tone with the last statement, "Ash, what's wrong? You don't sound happy about that. Is there something else we need to know?"

"Yeah, I just want to keep Wahaya out of it. I, umm, I asked if there was a way to turn him back to his human form.

Okon said he would ask the Spirits. I don't know if it's possible, but Mark, I want him to stay. I know it's crazy and fast and—"

"Ash, stop. I get it, and it's not that crazy. If there is a way to change him back, I'm sure they will. Hell, Shana and I kind of saw this coming. I mean, the guy brought you your favorite flower for God's sake, and you've always been a dog person," Mark replied while laughing at his own joke.

"Shana told you about the flowers?"

"No, she didn't. She did kind of hint about a gift and wanted me to watch out for you, but I noticed the flowers on the cooler he returned, earlier, when I passed your room, I saw fresh flowers in the vase on your chest of drawers. *Soooo*, since they're from higher on the mountain, I figured he brought them to you. You haven't left the lodge, except with Shana, and no one else brought you flowers. So, when I saw them, I asked Shana what your favorite flower was, and she confirmed what I suspected. There is only one person, well, creature, that would go that high on the mountain this time of year to get you flowers. I *am* a police officer, so I'm trained to notice things, you know. But how did he know they're your favorites?"

"I don't know. Maybe he just thought I would like them. I wasn't going to tell you all, but the first flowers he left were on my bed. Which meant he was in the lodge. That was the same night he came to me in his human form. The connection we had seemed to snap into place and became stronger that night, too. Kind of like it turned from a sewing thread into a ship's anchor rope. I'm not sure how to explain it, but if he stays, I'll be able to get to know him. See if this connection we have is real, or just some soul-bond from that other life that I was told of. Also, since he and I have this connection, what will happen if he were to be put back in slumber, I mean, to me at that point? Wouldn't you want to know?"

"Yes, I would. So, I hope things work out. But you need to do what you can to find out as much as possible in case things don't go your way. Promise?"

"I will... Promise. Now, what are you two up to this morning?"

Bidziil spoke up, "I'm not sure about Mark, but I will be joining the ritual. Tsali left me a message to join once I was up and had some water. So, I will not be back upstairs until we have accomplished the protection barrier, or if it takes longer, and we require a break. Please lock the basement door so that no one interrupts the ritual. We can't have any distractions."

With that, he headed downstairs. I followed him to the door and then locked it once he was out of sight. I walked back into the kitchen to Mark, pouring himself another cup of coffee, and asked if he could help with breakfast. I thought for a second, then suggested he rest a little more, and I'd let him know when the food was ready. He agreed and said he was going to lie on the couch since his friend, Stephenson, would arrive soon.

About thirty minutes later, I had brunch ready to go when there was another knock on the front door. Mark jumped up and went to look out the window, and was glad to see that his friend had made it. Mark went out and helped him unload his truck.

It seemed like his friend had also brought supplies of some sort. The stuff he brought was in military boxes, and I didn't feel like asking what it was or helping, because it looked really heavy. I figured we would know soon enough. I allowed myself to get lost in my thoughts while relocking the shutter

Mark looked out of. As they passed me, he tapped my shoulder, quickly introduced Stephenson, and nodded for Stephenson to keep going down the hall. They kept walking, and he said that he was going to take him to his room so he could put his stuff away. I nodded and said I'd see them later, and then went on to check the door. I didn't pay that much attention since I was still in my head. I went and woke Aunt Ulla, Shana, and Adohi, and then I returned to the kitchen and set the table.

I let everyone know that a ritual was taking place in the basement, and no one was allowed down there until the Elders requested either us or nourishment. All three nodded in unison, and I suggested they sit down for breakfast, and I would bring the food out. Adohi immediately sat down, while Shana and Aunt Ulla offered to help. I said they could clean up since I cooked. Mark walked in with his friend behind him.

I immediately noticed his friend was taller because I could see the top of his head slightly above Mark's. I went back into the kitchen to get the last of the dishes while Mark formally introduced his friend to everyone. Surprisingly, even Shana hadn't met him yet. As I walked back into the dining room, I went to set the food down, and I happened to look up to see Stephenson watching me.

I was shocked by his ruggedly handsome looks that almost matched Wahaya's—down to the scar in his right eyebrow. I couldn't help but stare for a moment.

Our eyes were locked until Mark cleared his throat, "Ashley, I'd like you to formally meet my old Marine buddy. This is Finlay Alexander Stephenson, but he prefers Alex or Stephenson. Stephenson, this is Shana's old college friend, Ashley, but we call her Ash."

He looked between the two of us, then snickered and asked if I needed any help bringing anything else from the kitchen.

"Umm, uh… no," I replied, "this was the last of it, but thank you. I hope you all are hungry. I got a little carried away wanting to make sure the three Elders also have plenty when they're ready to eat. So, umm, there's plenty… dig in."

As everyone served themselves, Stephenson and I locked eyes again, and I could swear a thread connection reached out and tangled with the one I shared with Wahaya. Stephenson's black eyes softened as he looked at me, and a slight smile crept in.

I watched as his mouth turned up into a tantalizing grin. He reminded me so much of Wahaya that I began to long for his kiss. I absent-mindedly touched my lips, remembering the passionate way he kissed me before he faded. I heard myself sigh and, realizing what I had done, I looked away from Stephenson's mouth to see everyone, but Adohi was looking at me. I smiled and acted as if nothing had happened, and asked Shana to pass the mashed potatoes.

I had made more dinner-type foods, but thankfully, no one said anything, and our meal was pretty uneventful, other than Shana glancing at me occasionally with a side-eye, and me trying to avoid looking at Stephenson as much as possible. We were all quiet as we ate, I was sure some of us were thinking about what might happen, while others were praying the protection ritual would work. Meanwhile, my thoughts were on Wahaya and how Alex could be his twin.

There was a noise from the kitchen, so I jumped up to head through the door when I suddenly felt a presence at my back. The next thing I knew, Alex stepped in front of me, "You stay back, I'll check it out."

Just then, Tsali called my name from the top of the basement stairs, "Miss Ashley, I need to talk with you."

I quickly moved in front of Alex, "Tsali, is everything okay? Do you all need something?"

"Everything is fine, Miss Ashley. We decided to take a short break to hydrate and give you a private update," he said, looking at Alex.

"Oh, um, sorry. Tsali, this is Alex Stephenson, and Alex, this is Tsali. He's one of the Elders working on the barrier. Did Mark tell you about what's going on?"

Not taking his eyes off Tsali, Alex answered, "Yeah, he explained everything. The Elders, the dogmen, and the scare tactics. I also noticed a few deep gashes in the trucks out front."

Tsali looked between Stephenson and me, then asked if we could speak in private. I agreed. Then we excused ourselves from the kitchen, and I took him up to my office. As soon as we walked in, he closed the door and spoke in a low tone, "How long have you known Mr. Stephenson?"

I shrugged, "Not long, an hour, maybe. He's Mark's friend from the military. Stephenson was a medic or something like that with Mark's special ops unit. I know he also dealt with some strange things while in the service. Why?"

Not answering my question, Tsali looked away, "Okon spoke with the spirits, as you asked. They told him the story of how a dogman was made and how to make him human again. They also said it might not work if the other half of its soul doesn't want it to work. At that time, the ritual would end, and the dogman would remain locked in that body forever, or it would die."

"Other half—what do you mean? Their souls are split and there's another half? Why didn't you tell me this before?"

"I am sorry, Miss Ashley. I know most of the lore, but not all. There were some things that the ancient Spirits had not shared until now. But what they told us was that when the dogmen were created, their souls were split. Half went into the creature, and the other was held in a type of limbo, in case the dogman went mad. This would possibly bring the warrior back and save the human side. Except for your Wahaya, when his soul split, it didn't go into limbo—instead, it went into a newborn that was dying. Consequently, the spirits said that the two pieces of his soul are here, near the lodge. His dogman form, and the descendant of the infant that received half of his soul. It appears that half has continued to reincarnate until the two halves could come together. The infant was Wahaya's sister's son. The ancient Spirits, the Elders, and I believe you just met Wahaya's other half of his soul."

"That sounds crazy. I mean—this whole thing is crazy, but this is the cherry on top of the crazy cake. So, let's say that this is all true. Did the spirits tell Okon how to change Wahaya back to human form?"

"Yes. The two souls will need to come together in a blood ritual-type ceremony. That is the only way other than for them to both die at the same time. Then the soul would be whole, but they would both be dead."

I started pacing. It helps me focus and keeps me calm, so I said, "Well, shit, what are we going to do? I could try to contact Wahaya and speak with him. He may not even want to be human again. What do you suggest?"

I looked up from my pacing to see Alex standing in the doorway. Apparently, Tsali heard the knock and opened the door. Tsali looked at both of us, then said, "I think you need to speak with both of them, possibly the human, first, since he is here." Then he walked out of my office, leaving me alone with Alex.

"How much of our conversation did you hear?"

"Enough. He was talking about how the creatures were made."

A bit annoyed that he had been listening, I asked, "You were eavesdropping? Why? Why did you come up here?"

Seeing that I was upset, he took a step toward me. Honestly, not the smartest thing to do, but then again, he didn't really know me.

"Your aunt asked someone to come up and get you. She said she needed to write out a schedule for sleeping shifts and a few other things. I volunteered. I didn't mean to listen in, and I didn't want to interrupt the two of you either, but when I heard my name, I wanted to know why you two were talking about me. Now, I'm not so sure I like what I heard."

"Yeah, me either. Let's go, and we can talk later. I don't want to keep my aunt waiting."

Walking past him, he lightly grabbed my arm, leaned in close, and said, "We need to figure this out soon, before the full moon. That's usually when big rituals take place." Before he let me go, he closed his eyes and took a deep breath, and had I not known better, I would have sworn it was Wahaya. A chill ran through me, and I walked away, leaving him to close the door.

Chapter 10

I was the first one scheduled to sleep while the men stayed alert and Shana sat with Adholi. My aunt said she was staying with me this time. Tsali, Bidziil, and Okon were back downstairs holding the barriers until daylight, then they would take a break to sleep and eat. Before Tsali went back downstairs, he agreed for me to get in touch with Wahaya, if possible, and see if I could talk to him about Soul Weaving.

I had no problem agreeing because I wanted to see him. There was a desire that had been building since I had allowed myself to open up to the possibilities and the desires. It was as if a flood of feelings and emotions came raging through. So, I let everyone know I was heading to my room and asked my aunt not to come up for a couple of hours. She wasn't happy with that but agreed anyway since she knew I had to make contact, and that might take some time.

Back in my room, I found myself drawn to the balcony doors. I looked out and there, in front of my door, were more flowers. I opened it, brought the flowers in, and quickly locked the door behind me. I glanced over to the woods across the pond, and I could see a figure hidden in the trees. He raised his paw to let me know he was there. I closed my eyes and focused on him. I sent him a message that I wanted to see him in my dreams. When I opened my eyes, he was gone. I could only hope he was able to come alone—*if* he was able to come. I wasn't sure if the barrier would keep him out or not. It was supposed to keep the others out mentally and physically.

Once I lay down, I started doing a relaxation technique to help me fall asleep, which didn't take long.

~

I was standing on my balcony, looking out towards the pond, when his arm wrapped around my waist. His other hand caressed my arm as he leaned down and whispered in my ear, "You called for me, my angel?"

I turned to face him and was stunned as I started to see the resemblance to Alex now, "Why are we on my balcony? Can you come inside with me?"

Smiling, he said, "The barrier has stopped them from coming near the dwelling or following me into your dreamtime. It was safer for me to come to you than to have you join me in the woods outside the barrier. And yes, if you want me to join you inside, I can."

I took his hand and led him into my room, locking the door behind us. Then I guided him to the bed for us to sit. He smiled, and it was a wickedly sexy smile, and my thoughts immediately went where his had gone when we sat down. He leaned in and kissed me, long and sensually. I returned the kiss for a moment but had to stop him.

"We need to talk about a few things while we can," I started, "I know now that you can come through the barrier, and they can't. I hope it holds until they can find a way to send the other dogmen back and break the connection to Mr. Skullthorn. But at the moment, I need to talk to you about something important. I'm not sure how to say this, so please bear with me and don't get upset, okay?"

He nodded his head and let me continue, "Well, I asked one of the Elders if there was a way to make you human again. He spoke with the Spirits, and they told him the story of how you were made and how to make you human again... that is— if you want to. It could be dangerous, and there are several ways it could go. But would you... want to be human again?"

I looked into his eyes to see warmth, and what I felt was a deep, soul love. A love that burned hotter than any fire ever could.

"Does that mean you want and accept me?" He asked. "If you do, then yes, I would. I would do whatever I must to be human again if it means I can be with you and not only in dreamtime. Yes, my angel. What will it take to do this?"

"That's where it gets tricky. So... um... apparently, when you were created, your soul was split in two. One half stayed with you, and the other half, somehow, was placed in your nephew, who was dying. For you to be human again, we would have to bring the two halves of your soul together, into one body."

His face dropped, and I knew what he was thinking, so I told him about Alex. "

I met him this morning—and I had to look twice because he looked that much like you. He even smells like you, and the connection or bond that you and I have—it was as if when he and I looked at each other, one formed with him too. It was almost like I felt you coming through him."

Apprehensively, he smiled, "Are you sure he has the other half of my soul? I will need to see him myself. Please ask the Elders to confirm and sanctify that it is truly the other half. I am sure they will have a way. Then he will have to agree to the ritual, as well, yes?"

"He overheard Tsali and I talking, so he knows, but I wanted to talk to you first. Because you both have to agree and want it to happen, for it to work. I will talk with him again, too, and let you know. But for you to see him, it will have to be at a distance since the other two are around still. I'll bring him out onto my balcony today. Will that work?"

"Yes, my vision and hearing in my dogman form are enhanced. But for now, while we have time, I want more of you."

He leaned in and kissed me again, except this time, the kiss was filled with yearning and more passion than before. I didn't fight it; I allowed myself to feel the passion, and we melted together.

He began trailing kisses down my jawline as he tore open my nightshirt. He trailed his kisses down until he reached my right nipple. His tongue began circling, and flicking my bud which quickly rose for him to suck. All I could do was moan and pull him closer. Then I felt his hand trailing lightly down my body, reaching its destination where he inserted a finger. He hummed with pleasure against my breast as he realized I was wet and ready for him.

As he moved to tease my other nipple, he added another finger, slowly sliding in and out, setting a rhythm that built and intensified my pleasure, only to have him stop. Then he torturously trailed tender nibbles and sucking kisses down my stomach to my folds, where his tongue found its intended target - circling, flicking, and joining his fingers in the dance of moving in and out, increasing the heat. Then he began to lightly suck on my nub and I almost came only to have him go back to lightly kissing and licking my sweet spot.

The ballet of feelings that danced through my body rose to a crescendo. His endeavors were quickly rewarded, and my climax hit full force. He enjoyed my juices as though he was drinking from the fountain of life. The pleasure that surged through me was the strongest I'd ever had—in reality or dreams. As I slowly calmed from my orgasm, he kissed his way back up, retracing his original path all the way to my mouth. I could taste myself on his lips. I held his gaze, still breathless. And kissed him tenderly.

I suddenly realized that he was more solid than his usual dream form.

"You know this is the longest we've been able to be together?" I asked. "You usually fade out. Do you know why that happens?"

But before he could answer, he began to melt away as there was a knock at my door.

His ghost kissed me goodbye.

~

I huffed, and with my eyes still closed, I yelled, "Damn it! Come in!" I slowly opened my eyes, and I noticed my aunt or Shana wasn't in my room yet. Then there was another knock.

So, I guess when I yelled "come in," it was in my head. Maybe I am going crazy...

This time, I yelled out loud. "Come on in!"

As I got up, I realized I was wet from Wahaya's fruitful endeavors. My nightshirt was, in fact, torn as if it weren't a dream. Just as I stood, Alex walked in. When he saw me, he stopped and stared.

"I—um, you said to come in. I can go," He stammered as he stared. The look on his face spoke of a desire I had only seen before—on Wahaya. Alex's eyes darkened, and his breath sped up as he tried to turn away but kept failing.

I grabbed some clothes and hurried toward the bathroom. As I passed him, I shook my head, "No, it's fine, and I said come in. I'll go get dressed in the bathroom. We kind of need to talk anyway. Please, shut the door."

I needed a shower but... oh what the hell—I jumped in for a quick wash-off. Then I got dressed and, as I opened the bathroom door, I saw Alex standing out on the balcony. There was a flash from my dream with Wahaya, and I started to feel heated again.

Sensing me behind him, Alex turned around and asked me to join him. He pointed to the other side of the lake at a figure standing near a tree, "Is that the dogman that visits you?"

I smiled and nodded, "Yes," I replied, "That's Wahaya. I spoke with him about the ritual, and he has some questions, but he doesn't not want to do it. Mainly he wanted to see you and, well, now he has seen you, and you him."

Alex didn't take his eyes off Wahaya's dogman form as he took a deep breath, "I felt a pull to come out here. Guess that explains it. Him, wanting to see me, I mean. This is all really strange, but if we share a soul, I suppose we might sense each other. Possibly even share other things."

I was still looking at Wahaya across the lake when my breathing started to pick up. I began to feel heat forming in my core again. I looked at Alex, knowing the answer but asked anyway, "Other things? Like what?"

Still not looking at me, he went on to say, "Like being attracted to you, feeling there is something unexplainable between us. I felt it as soon as I saw you. Maybe even before I got here. When Mark called and asked for my help, I knew I had to come, and that this would be a life-changing experience. Not just because of the dogmen or the other stuff happening here. I've seen and dealt with things like that before. I mean, there's some fucked up shit out there that the majority of people don't know about and would freak out if they did. But this was different. I… I knew you and I can't explain what's happening now."

He turned to look at me instead of at the lake and stepped closer, bringing his large hand up to cup my cheek. His hand was rough yet comforting—warm and tender. He looked at my eyes, then my lips, then leaned down and kissed me.

At first, I was caught off guard, but his kiss grew hungry, and I couldn't help myself. I answered his kiss with an intensity I'd only shared with one other. I would have sworn it was Wahaya kissing me.

Then I heard a loud howl that cut through the air. We both stopped, lips still together, trying to catch our breath. Separating, we turned to the woods to see that Wahaya was now standing at the edge of the lake. I felt his pain at seeing me return Alex's kiss.

I heard his voice in my head saying, "Mine, not just in dreams!" Then he howled as he turned and walked into the woods with his head down. Then he turned, looked at Alex, and I could have sworn he gave him a nod.

"He didn't like me kissing you, did he? I'm not sorry, though, I… I had no control."

Taking a slight step back, I answered with a slight smirk, "He didn't, but he did at the same time. I think he now knows that you have the other half of his soul. He may have even influenced the kiss, some, I can't confirm that, but I wouldn't be surprised."

Alex opened the balcony door for us to go back in, then he locked it and pulled the curtains closed. He turned back to me as he came closer and said, "This one is all me," and then he kissed me again.

The kiss was powerful, full of desire and passion. As he kissed me, I felt the heat in my core come alive again and—

Damn, I would need another shower.

Again, I surrendered, and one kiss melted into another, each increasing the heat between us so much we could have started a fire. Then—damn it—my aunt knocked on the door.

She cleared her throat and asked, "Ashley, is Alex in there with you? Mark needs his help with something, and Shana wanted to know if you could stay with Adohi while she gets some rest. I'm also fixing some snacks for everyone."

I tried to catch my breath and smiled into his lips as he kept kissing me. He began to trail his kisses down my jawline to my neck, where he began lightly sucking. He and Wahaya had a thing for kissing my neck. God bless, if it wasn't for my aunt at the door, I swear this shirt would've been ripped off as well. My nipples were already trying to push through my bra, and I was definitely wet for more.

But my aunt *was* at the door. Even though I wanted to finish this, I cleared my throat before answering, "Yes, Aunt Ulla, I gave him a little project. He's almost done, so we'll be right there. We'll see you downstairs, okay?"

He'd moved back up to kiss my lips, so I put my hands on both sides of his face and reluctantly pulled him away, whispering, "We need to go downstairs, because if we keep this up, Mark won't have your help anytime soon. So, I'm going to head to the bathroom to freshen up, again, alone. While you, um, calm yourself so you can see what Mark needs. Okay?" I glanced down to see that he was as ready as I was, and it looked like he was likely just as well-endowed as Wahaya.

He stepped back and looked like he had just woken up from a dream. His eyes seemed to have turned an even darker black from desire. He took a deep breath to calm himself and muttered, "I, umm, couldn't stop and, honestly, I still don't want to. But you're right, we need to go downstairs before I have to taste more of you." He was smirking as he adjusted himself before heading to the door.

I looked over my shoulder to catch him smiling.

I don't think Wahaya had anything to do with that kiss, regardless, with my eyes closed, I don't think I could really tell them apart. Dreams and reality are starting to blur and since Alex reminds me so much of Wahaya—it's a little confusing.

I quickly freshened up and saw that Alex had already gone, so I went to join them downstairs.

Chapter 11

Shana saw me and immediately had a glint in her eyes as she told me what was going to happen, "Ashley, I'm headed upstairs to get some rest. Adohi is playing a game at the moment, sooooo, you have time to come talk with me for a bit before I take a nap. We need some girl time, and I'm dying to know what's been going on. Your aunt mentioned Alex was in your room and then went to fix snacks for everyone. Mark and Alex are currently working on something in the mudroom area, and the Elders are all downstairs keeping the ritual flowing. So, let's go upstairs now!"

We laughed so hard we almost tripped over the first step as we flew up to her and Mark's room.

Once we were settled, sitting on her bed with wine, Shana looked at me and said, "Spill, Chicky, there is way too much intense shit going on here. I could use something else to think about, and you've had a glow since you came back downstairs. So, spill!"

I rolled my eyes and laughed to hide the blush I could already feel reaching my cheeks. But I knew she would not relent, and I needed to talk things out to keep myself sane. So, I told her everything—from my talks with Tsali, to the first meeting with Alex, the dream with my passionate Wahaya, and then to what happened with Alex on the balcony, and after. I told her how confused I was, but that I had come to a realization.

"Shana, I think I figured out how, or why, Wahaya fades when he does. I think he senses when someone is coming, and that automatically triggers the fade. Because no sooner than he fades, there is either a knock on my door or one of you calls my name. But one thing that has me stumped, when I opened my eyes from this last dream... my nightshirt was *ripped*. I wouldn't have thought it would have been ripped in reality, would you? Oh, and he didn't fade as fast this time, but I wonder if that was because it was Alex."

Shana took on a serious look. I had given her something to think about that didn't have to do with danger. I could see in her expression that she had an idea. Shana made her thinking face with her nose scrunched up and said, "What if— and this is way out there, so you can definitely throw it out if you think I'm so far off—but, what if it wasn't a dream? What if he has the ability to fade into, not only your dreams, but reality? Like your room or wherever you're at? I mean, we don't know all that they can do, and we *are* dealing with beings that we never thought existed before, so, what if he can?"

I thought about it for a moment, then agreed, "It could be possible, and it would explain the ripped shirt. But if Wahaya can do that, I wonder if the others can too? Oh God, Adohi!"

Coming to the same conclusion, Shana and I jumped up and ran downstairs nonstop to Adohi's room, where he was still deep into game mode. At least, until we burst through his door. He looked up at us like we were crazy. Shana and I looked at each other and were relieved that there were no monsters in his room—other than those in his game. Since Adohi was safe, we were free to laugh as hard as we wanted. We leaned against the wall, trying to control our laughing spell.

After we stopped, I said, "Shana, you need to go get some rest. I'll get a few things together to keep me busy while spending time with our gamer here, and I'll let the guys know that we may have figured out that Wahaya might be able to fade into reality and that we hope the others can't."

She agreed, and we both left. She headed upstairs, and I went to grab some snacks, my tablet, and then hit the bathroom. On my way back, I stopped to let Mark and Alex know what Shana and I thought might happen with the fading. The whole time I was talking, I tried not to look at Alex, but I couldn't help peeking his way, only to see him staring at me.

Damn, the heat that radiated off him... even from the other side of the table was fire hot. Again, I've only felt this type of pull and heat with Wahaya. If I were even a little bit uncertain about them sharing a soul, or DNA, or whatever, the way their similarities keep growing would take the doubts away.

Wait a minute, DNA?

"Alex," I said, "Do you have any Native American, Cherokee, or maybe Mountain Tribe blood?"

Hesitantly, he gave me a slight smirk, "Yes, my mother was three-quarters or more, I believe it was Cherokee. My father is Scottish." He added, with a more devious smile, "Is there anything else I can help you with?"

I knew exactly what he was saying. I felt flushed and cleared my throat a bit louder than I thought. Mark looked between the two of us with a chuckle before asking, "Ash, isn't your mother's family also Cherokee or from the mountain?"

"Yes, they are. From this area, actually. Um, I need to go sit with Adohi, especially if it's possible for the fade in and out thing to happen beyond dreams. Excuse me." I turned so quickly, and I almost ran into the door, and I heard Mark snicker behind me.

Damn it!

I quickly made it back to Adohi's room to find him still deep in his game. I set our snacks and drinks down, then picked up a controller, motioning that I'd play with him. He saved his game, and we started a new one. We played for several rounds.

Before I knew it, Shana was knocking and coming in.

"Are you ready for a break?" she asked, "You've been in here for at least four hours. Have either of you napped or eaten?"

"Snacks are gone, but we've been playing pretty much the whole time," I replied. "Well, except for potty breaks, but I'm ready to stand up and stretch, move around. You want to take over? Adohi, it looks like the sun's out, so you might want to get some sleep too."

He agreed, though he decided he wanted to have a sandwich first. So, he put his controllers up, and the three of us went for food. When we got to the kitchen, the three Elders, along with my aunt, Mark, and Alex, were gathered around the table talking. As I walked in, they all looked up with serious expressions, and my aunt made room for me to sit down.

"What's going on?" I asked, "You're all so serious. Are the barriers holding?"

Bidziil stood up and started walking around, "Miss Ashley, the barriers are holding for now. We are only taking a break to eat, take a respite, and... talk to you. We... we have spoken to the ancient Spirits, and they have directed us regarding what needs to be done to break the hold on the dogmen and to change your Wahaya back to his human form."

Tsali took over at this point, turning to look at me, "Did you speak to Wahaya?"

"Yes," I answered. "He said he wanted you to make sure that Alex has the other half of his soul. Then he kind of confirmed it after we spoke." I glanced at Alex and smiled, then I continued, "He said he wants to do whatever he needs to do to be human again, whether it means sharing a body, or that he might not make it. He wants to try."

Bidziil nodded his head lightly, "We confirmed with the Spirits that Alex has the other half of the Wahaya's soul. We have also spoken with Alex about everything. How things may change in his life. The Ancients wanted to make sure he was prepared for unexpected things that might happen. We have given him more than enough information to make a decision when he is ready. Although we are running short on time.

"Once we have everything ready for the rituals, we will need you to be present. The first ritual is to break the hold and hopefully send the others back, while simultaneously bringing Wahaya and Alex's soul halves together into one. We were assured that the whole soul would only go into the human. I suggest you get as much rest as possible and let Wahaya know the ritual will take place tomorrow at sunset. If Alex agrees. Wahaya will need to be on the property, but we will have to drop the shield to perform both rituals, so everyone will need to be downstairs, including... Wahaya. Let him know that he will need to control his inner creature. You will go into a dream state, which we will assist you with, right before the ceremony, so you can let him know when and where to come before we begin."

"Wow! Okay, I was headed to get some sleep anyway, so I'll call out to him and let him know. Hmm... thank you, and please thank the Spirits for me too. Ahh, Alex, could I talk to you for a moment, please?"

He stood up and followed me out, and I didn't stop. I went straight to my room, and once we were in, I closed the door.

"Have you thought about this, I mean, seriously thought about it. Are you sure you want to do this? Things could get crazy, and you don't know me. Wahaya is determined that he will be with me, and we do have a connection, and yes, I feel the same type of connection with you, but if you don't—"

Before I could say anything else, he grabbed me and kissed me, shutting me up immediately. Our kiss was long and hot, it ignited my body and soul. Once we came up for air, he looked at me and then kissed my forehead and said, "My life has been nothing but existing, you are tied to not only his half of our soul, but to mine too. I dreamt of you when I was in the service. I feel that connection again now, and I want a life with you. True, we don't know a lot about each other, but what fun it will be getting to know each other. Plus, I know more about you than you think. Mark's been trying to introduce us for a while, so he told me quite a bit about you. In my heart, I think I knew it was you from my dreams. Mark never showed me a picture, but I felt it was you. And when he called me to come help, I knew this would change my life. So, don't worry, I know what I'm doing, and I want this. Whether I've known you for five minutes or a lifetime... I want this, because I want... Hello, I need to be with you. You are my future one way or another."

He kissed me again, then turned and left me standing there wanting more, all while telling me to get some sleep and that he would see me later. How was I going to sleep now?

I took a deep breath as I changed into a nightshirt and climbed into bed. Surprisingly, I fell asleep as I was debating whether I should have taken a shower first.

~

Steam fogged the mirror as I stood at my bathroom sink. I leaned forward to clear a spot on the mirror. My towel slipped to the floor, and I heard a deep growl behind me. I slowly turned to see Wahaya in his dogman form. He stepped out of the doorway into the steam of the bathroom, and as he moved in front of me, he changed into his human self. His body heat added to the steam encircling me.

"You were thinking of me, I came to please," his deep voice, wrapped in velvet, struck a chord within me. I didn't remember calling out to him, at least not yet, but my body and soul seemed to reach out to him with the thread of our connection humming louder the closer he drew.

He reached out and pulled me to him, and his skin was hot against mine. He lowered his mouth to mine in a slow and teasing kiss. . He nibbled my bottom lip and sucked on my tongue. This kiss quickly turned claiming and devouring in a powerful moment. He kissed me like a starved man, desperate to remember what it meant to taste, to claim, to hold.

Our passion ignited like a fire fueled by kerosene, unburdened by clothes, nothing between us but steam and raw desire. Feeling his arousal—thick, hard, and pulsing against my skin, I ached for him—body, soul, essence—like I'd been starving for years and only he could satiate me. His kisses became primal and hungry. As he lifted me, I wrapped my legs around his waist. My breath caught as he turned, carrying me to my bed. As he laid me down, our kisses grew more demanding, desperate, pleading for more.

"I've waited, but no more. I need you, all of you." His voice was deep as he growled against my neck. Filled with desire, his mouth claimed mine, devouring my return kiss. He began moving across my jaw line, and he nipped at my ear lobe just hard enough for me to gasp. Covering me with his heat, his hands traveled over me as if he were memorizing every inch with his touch. Slow and possessive, every inch of me that he touched sparked to life with fire. His mouth found my breast—he licked, sucked, and teased until I was moaning his name like a prayer, pulling him closer.

His hands slipped between my thighs, finding the treasure he wished to claim. Two fingers glided inside me, pulsing to a rhythm that only he and I danced to. He teased me to the edge again, and again while he kissed his way down to taste the juices he teased from me. Once his tongue found my nub, he began to suck and lick, causing such torturous pleasure. I wanted to taste him, but he was set on savoring every sound I made, relishing each tremble in my thighs.

My orgasm came hard, and he drank from me like I was a fountain, then he hummed, "Mmmm, you are so wet and ready for me. I have dreamt of you over and over, lying under me, taking me in."

"Please, no more teasing, I need you!" I begged.

He entered me slowly—so agonizingly slow I thought I would die with anticipation. I tried moving to bring him in deeper, but he held me tight, and then in one movement, he filled me. He stretched me with his heat and pressure that was more than physical. Our union was spiritual, like our bodies and souls were designed for one another. We were pieces of a puzzle that fit perfectly together.

He began moving his hips with a primal rhythm that I hungrily matched. Our bodies ground against our aching. Our breaths tangled, moans rising while our bodies met time and time again. Harder, deeper, locking us together in a mystical dream. The air was wild and ancient. Each movement brought us closer, and my vision flickered of our union in another life together, confirming that we were destined.

Our bodies came together in a blinding climax. We shattered together, locked in place as wave, after wave, of pleasure surged through us. We called out each other's names, tying our souls together eternally.

Our breaths were ragged as we finally stilled. He pulled me close, and we held each other tightly. His breath was warm on my breast where his head lay. He tenderly kissed my skin, then looked up at me, "I love you—in this life and any other. Once my soul is whole, even if it is in another man's body, it will still be me. I will find a way to let you know I am still with you."

I kissed him with an understanding I felt deep in my heart, "I didn't think I would ever feel this way or so soon, but I love you, and you'd better find a way to let me know you're there."

We kissed, and all of a sudden, I could feel coolness taking over the air. As I opened my eyes, he began disappearing into a mist. Only then did I remember what I was supposed to tell him, "Oh my God! I almost forgot. Umm, tomorrow, I will call you, and you need to come in your dogman form to the lodge. I'll meet you at the back door. We'll be doing the ceremony then. Please don't kill anyone in the house."

With a smile, he nodded, and within a few seconds, only his scent and the feeling of his touch lingered.

~

There was a loud banging on my door. I opened my eyes as Alex burst through, "I've been trying to wake you for the last ten minutes!"

I jumped up, trying to decide what to do first, and I looked up to see him staring at me again. I felt like Deja Vu, and as I looked into his eyes that had grown dark with desire, I smirked, "You're developing a habit of coming in when I'm... half dressed." I opened my arms wide to prove my point. I knew I was pushing his control to its limits, but I didn't care. I stood I knew I was pushing his control to its limits, but I didn't care. I stood in front of him almost completely naked. I was on display for the desire in his eyes.

Surprisingly, I did have on a pair of white lace panties dotted with pink hearts. Not sure how those appeared, but they were still wet from Wahaya. The look on Alex's face was filled with—

What is it... a mix of desire, lust, and... is that fear? That was a brief flash of fear, but what is he scared of... me... but why?

Not thinking, I stepped closer to Alex and reached out to him. "What's wrong? Did something happen? Is everyone okay? Are you okay?"

"Everything is fine, I'm... umm, I'm fine, just... admiring the view."

"Are you sure everything is fine? You looked... I don't know, fearful, and something else, I'm may be wrong, but..." I had now ruined the playful mood I had started.

He moved a step closer, "I wouldn't call it fear, it was more like recognition. There's an ancient part of me that feels like it's humming or vibrating with the knowledge that we were meant to be together. Like you've always been a part of me, but never mine, and that scares the hell out of me. I want you, and seeing you like this makes controlling myself extremely hard."

He lightly kissed me on the cheek and hurriedly turned to leave. Looking back over his shoulder, he told me the food was ready, then walked through the door and shut it. Leaving me staring at the closed door.

Chapter 12

I was feeling refreshed and ready for whatever was going to happen by the time I joined the others downstairs. Everyone sat at the dining room table, talking and snacking. I said good morning, sarcastically a little too happily, as I went into the kitchen to get some coffee. Shana came in behind me with a huge shit-eating grin on her face and leaned over the counter, "Sooooo... did Alex help you get up?"

"What? No! He just... ummm, caught me getting out of bed—half-dressed after Wahaya left." Shana's question hit me the wrong way, and it was apparent in my tone. I knew she could tell.

Taking on a less playful tone, Shana asked, "Oh no! I'm sorry, Ash... what happened? Tell me. There's so much crazy shit happening here—I didn't mean to upset you. I just wanted some hot fun info to help balance it. Please tell me!"

I quickly let go of the attitude; it wasn't her fault I was grumpy. "Well... I was coming out of, umm, a sex dream with Wahaya... and I have to tell you, I have never, ever had such a strong orgasm before! It was amazing, romantic, and... well... anyway, as he faded, I heard pounding on my door, and the next thing I knew, Alex was standing in my room. I jumped up, and, well..."

"Well?"

I laughed a little, then continued, "Well... I was naked except I had on my pink heart lace panties. Not to mention, they were sex-wet, and I'm sure he might have been able to smell my arousal. So... nothing after that. He just stared for a few seconds, then kissed me on the cheek and told me there was food ready. Oh—and that he had been trying to wake me for about ten minutes. Then he turned and left. Which means, he probably heard me too."

"Crap, that's so hot. Has anything else happened that you haven't told me about? I mean, we haven't had any real girl time since yesterday. Things are happening so fast for you." She had a mischievous grin and sparkle in her eyes as she talked.

"Well, I think I told you this already. Damn, I hate that my days are getting so screwed up, but... Wahaya wanted to see him, and before I could tell Alex, he went on my balcony, and it was like Wahaya was able to take over him—kind of. Anyway, he kissed me on the balcony. You may have heard Wahaya howl. I think he was half upset yet pleased that they're connected. Then Wahaya left, and Alex and I went back into my room, and he kissed me again. It's possible that Wahaya was still in control—but not fully—but Alex was fully in. Shana—kissing him was like kissing Wahaya, and it's weird. They smell alike, taste alike... God, I hope they do other things alike too once the ritual is completed. Which—I need to talk to Tsali about and find out what the plan is and when we're doing this."

I snapped my fingers to get her attention because she was somewhere else. "Shana, Sha...na! Hello!"

"Oh! Sorry. I was thinking about how hot it would be—taking Mark into the woods and having my way with him. He's been so focused on protecting us that he's only given me quick pecks here and there. Hearing your dream and feeling the heat coming off you and Alex when you're in the same room is just... well, it's frustrating for me. Which is going to be really good for Mark."

Shana started laughing, and then we both got the giggles. She was so tickled that she snort-laughed, which made us both laugh even harder. Next thing we knew, Mark and Alex walked in looking at us like we were crazy, which made us laugh even harder. Now I had to pee and, apparently, so did Shana. We crossed our legs in kind of a pee-pee dance as we giggled our way past the boys, and both went running, each to a different bathroom. I barely noticed that the guys had followed us out, and I heard my aunt start laughing, too.

When Shana and I walked back into the dining room, we had composed ourselves for the most part until we looked at each other, and we tried not to get into another giggle fit. Then we looked at the table and saw Mark, and that did it for us.

Through laughter, Shana said she was going to check on Adohi, and I said I was going to finally get my coffee. I heard my aunt tell them that Shana and I used to get the giggles together, especially when we shared secrets that only we found funny. As I came out of the kitchen with a huge mug, I saw Mark heading toward Adohi's room to find Shana. Mark has always loved a good secret—possibly part of his law enforcement training. I had to smile as I knew what he had in store once he found her.

A minute later, out of the corner of my eye, I noticed Mark and Shana slip up the stairs to their room. I looked down at my coffee to hide my smile because I knew they would be MIA for a while. Then I heard my name—I looked up and saw Alex. His eyes were waiting on mine, and I wanted to disappear with him to see if he *was* Wahaya incarnate. Then I heard my name again. This time, it was Tsali.

"Sorry, Tsali," I said, "I was lost in, mmm… thought. What did you say?"

"Miss Ashley, were you able to talk to Wahaya and let him know what is happening today?" Tsali asked again.

As I answered, I could feel the heat of a blush burning my cheeks. "Kind of. I was able to tell him I would call him and that he needed to come in his dogman form to the back of the lodge—and not to kill any of us when we let him in. It was hurried, and he was in mid-phase, so I hope he got it."

Tsali noticed the blush across my cheeks, but he didn't ask why I didn't tell Wahaya before he faded. Instead, he chose to ignore that comment and went into details for later.

"Oh, okay. Well... let us hope he comes when you call. We need to get started once the Elder is ready. He said to give him two hours, so we have at least an hour left. The only thing you can bring to the ritual is water. The Elder will need to draw blood from you, Alex, and Wahaya in his dogman form. You will make the cut on Wahaya's paw, and Alex's hand, then I will make the cuts on both of yours. You will stand facing me with the two of them facing you. Wahaya will be first. There will be things happening in between each binding cut, so don't turn to the other until I tell you. While the Elder, you, and I are performing this Soul Rejoining ritual, Bidziil will be preparing items for the next ritual, where we sever the connection between the other two dogmen and Skullthorn. Since we do not know how the Soul Rejoining will go, and if one, or both, will... um, be part of the Purging and Banishment ritual, we will need you to work with us on that ritual as well. We will need as many of you as possible."

Mark and Shana came back in time to hear about the second ritual. Both of them said they were ready to help, however needed. Tsali let Mark know that he would need to keep watch, but Shana, Aunt Ulla, and Adohi would need to be within the ceremonial circle. He went on to explain what they would do while both ceremonies took place. While Tsali explained the process of what everyone would be doing, I sat and picked at my food, thinking about the last few days.

I was lost in thought for what felt like forever until I heard Tsali tell me I had a short amount of time left if I wanted to do anything before the ritual. I looked up, acknowledging that I heard him, then headed into the kitchen to get a pitcher of water to take downstairs. Alex followed me, grabbing my hand as I opened the pantry door.

"Ashley," he said, "before you call for him, I wanted to talk to you. I wanted to reassure you that I'm all in—regardless of the outcome and that I've enjoyed meeting you. I don't know if it will be me or... well, you know, not me once it's all done. I wish I'd met you before all of this. I would have liked to have more time with you as me."

"I would have liked that too," I said, "But are you positive you want to do this? As I said earlier, you don't owe me anything, and you have a life of your own, which will mostly change once this is done."

"Ashley, I don't have a life, and I haven't had one for an extremely long time." He stepped closer to me and put his hands on both sides of my face, lifting it so I was looking straight into his eyes, our lips almost touching.

"I've known since I was young that I was missing something. During my military time, I was so good at what I did because I was not a whole man. I may have been part of the medical team, but I dealt with other dark things as well. I've lived off the grid for so long that being around people is... loud, and I usually can't stand it. But being here with this group has made me see I want more, being near you is what I want...As I said earlier, you are a part of me. I've known you, and I don't want to be without you anymore. I want to be with you anyway possible, and I'll take whatever I'm blessed to have, and however I can be with you. Either with me or not, but I can't live without you anymore. You are my missing half, and I know a part of me will be with you."

Before I could say anything, he kissed me, hard, and it was filled with longing, desire, and a lifetime of need all rolled into one. His tongue was hot and demanding. I answered with as much passion and heat as he gave me. Our kiss was turning into more very quickly.

Without thinking, we instinctively stepped inside the pantry and shut the door, continuing our heated kissing. His hands began mapping my body like he wanted to be able to remember every inch. He slipped my t-shirt up over my head, pulled my bra down, and began kissing and sucking my nipples. He moved back up to my lips, claiming me as we kept kissing. I could feel the heat traveling between my thighs. He began to move his mouth down to suck on my nipples again, while he pulled my leggings down and slipped a finger between my folds.

His voice hummed against my skin, "God, you are so wet, I want you—all of you." He added another finger, going deeper and curling one to find my G-spot. I felt my orgasm mounting, then he stopped sucking my nipple as he moved down so that he could lick and tease my clit while pumping his fingers in and out of me.

I could barely breathe, let alone speak, but managed to tease out, "Alex... *please*... I want... you... in me... now, please... I need you!"

He stood up as he undid his belt and jeans, dropped them down to his ankles, and without any words, he positioned himself and pushed up into me in one swift movement, causing me to gasp. He felt huge. He picked me up and put my back against the wall without shelves. I wrapped my legs around his waist, pulling him deeper as we began a rhythm—

slow at first, then our pace quickened as our kisses grew in urgency. He pinched one of my nipples with a sharp tug that sent fire racing to my core, and my orgasm exploded in waves. He pulled me tighter as his own release tore free. My body gripped him with hungry spasms, demanding all of him. I clutched him tighter, deepening our kiss. I wanted all of him, every drop.

As we came down from our ecstasy, we staggered a little, breathing hard, as he rested his head on my shoulder, feathering kisses to my collarbone.

"Alex," I started, "as much as I hate to stop—and I really would like to take this upstairs and repeat over, and over—we need to get ready for the ceremonies."

"I know. And you need to shower to remove my scent, or else he may kill me before the ritual does. If he smells me on you, he'll be deadly. Sharing a soul or not. I should've thought of that, but... I've felt that I might not get a chance to be with you, and the desire took over. The connection we have still scares the shit out of me... but I know this made our bond stronger. I wanted you when I dreamt of you, and then when I saw you coming out of the kitchen, the need only grew stronger. Hell, when I walked in the lodge and got a glimpse of the back of you, I felt something. And after our first kiss, I knew... we were to be together. I had to be with you, as me, at least once. This ritual can go in several directions, and I might not be the one to come out of it, so forgive me for being selfish, but I had to be with you. I know this is crazy, but I love you, Ashley."

I slowly kissed him, "I know. I've felt it too. And, surprisingly, both of you *are* one. Take it from me—if anyone would know, it's me. We have to believe in the ceremony, the Elders, all of it. We have to have faith that everything will turn out for both of you. Now, as you said, I need to shower, and we don't have much time. I think you need to shower as well, or he'll smell me... on... you." I kissed him sweetly while releasing my legs from around his waist, and he reluctantly released his hold so we could both get dressed.

"Oh, and Alex... I love you too."

We quietly peeked out the pantry door to see that the kitchen was empty, so we slipped out. I gave him a quick kiss, then we headed to our separate rooms to shower. Once in my room, I went to the balcony to look for Wahaya, but I didn't linger since I had to shower. I just couldn't scrub Alex off my skin. So I only rinsed off and put on clean clothes. It felt important to have both of them within me. Once I was done, I ran downstairs feeling scared and excited all rolled into one.

Tsali met me at the bottom of the stairs and, without talking, walked with me through the kitchen and out to the back porch. We stood on the deck staring out at the lake. It was a shame what was going on and that we couldn't truly enjoy our beautiful surroundings. I had forgotten how purely beautiful a snow-covered mountain scene could be. I wish I'd thought to bring my camera out and take some photos before... whatever is going to happen - happens. I closed my eyes as I took in a deep, crisp breath and slowly let it out. I re-opened my eyes and took in the most beautiful sight I'd ever seen. We had just been hit by another wave of the snowstorm, so the fresh powdered snow was covering everything. It was still untouched except where some of us had gone to get wood from the barn, and where we were now standing. Wish I had my camera or at least my phone.

Tsali brought me back to reality, "Miss Ashley, before you call Wahaya, I need to let you know what might happen tonight. First, I know you have been with both Mr. Alex and

Wahaya." As he saw the shock on my face, he quickly continued, "The Elders and Spirits are pleased that it happened. We could not have asked you to do that, but since it happened naturally, it is good. Even though you were with Wahaya in your dreamtime, you still have his seed within you, and it has now been joined by Mr. Alex's. This unites them within you, as will their blood during the ceremony. The three of you have been united in mind, soul, and now body... which will add the power that we will need. Now, it is time to call for Wahaya. Let him know it is time to come to the basement door. We will let him in, but he must keep control of his beast no matter what happens. Do you understand?"

"Yes, I'll make sure he knows that. Do you think he'll be upset that I was with, umm, Alex?"

"Possibly, but let him know it will make the ritual within the ceremony much stronger. If he is still upset, you will need to be prepared to calm him in any way possible. They both must be calm for this to work."

"I'll do what I can. I guess you'd better go and join the others. I'll be down there shortly. Oh, should I come through the house or come in with Wahaya, in the back?"

"Give me a few moments to go in and unlock the outer door, then you walk down and call him from there. That way, if there are any issues, you will be able to step into the basement quickly, or we can come to assist you if necessary. I will be watching, and the moment he is at the line, we will drop the barrier, but only long enough for him to cross into the lodge. I feel all will be fine. Now, I will see you shortly."

"Tsali, wait—I have a quick question. Umm, Adohi... with his leg and one of the bad dogmen having a sort of blood connection, should he be part of the ritual? Is it safe?"

He paused to think for a moment, then he looked at me and said, "Adohi is a strong young man and has more strength than even he knows. His leg is healing nicely, and he should be fine for the amount of time it will take. Plus, we have a chair set behind him in case he needs to sit down. As for his connection with Skullthorn's dogman, the barrier will be back in place in time, and we have some special herbs placed around Adohi to add a little extra protection. So, everything will be fine."

Tsali smiled, nodded, and went back in. Within a few minutes, I heard the click of the basement door unlatch. I slowly walked toward the steps leading to the outside landing. I looked over at the woods on the other side of the lake, and—standing in all his glory—there was Wahaya watching me. As I stood in front of the door, he moved quickly towards the lodge. I closed my eyes and called out to him and spoke the words Tsali had told me to say. Then I opened my eyes and realized I was looking straight into the amber eyes of my dogman.

I took in a sharp breath as I realized he wasn't even standing up yet. He was on all fours with his nose level to mine. He sniffed me and then growled. I could only assume he smelled Alex, so I hesitantly reached out to stroke his fur. He flinched a little but then leaned into my hand. I couldn't help but move closer. With my forehead to his, my hands came up to stroke his fur while I spoke to him, "Please, don't be angry. He is part of you, and it will help with the soul binding. I wish I could have known you in this form as well, my love. But it's time for the ritual. They asked that you come in as you are now and to keep control of your beast and temper, no matter what goes on. Remember, you and Alex are one, so please don't attack him. Okay?"

I moved back to look him in the eyes, and I saw sadness there. He bowed his head and mentally spoke to me, "I am yours no matter what form I am in. I only ask that you please remember me when I am no longer. I will be calm for you, my angel."

I kissed him on his muzzle, and a tear rolled down my cheek. He leaned into me as I hugged him and said, "I won't have to remember you, because you'll be here. No matter what form you are in, you'll be here. You are my warrior, I am yours from the past and now. You will never again be without me. I know that in my heart."

I moved my hand to my heart, then back through his fur, and I kissed him again. My heart was racing. Here was this huge, deadly creature that could take me out in one breath, but instead, he loves me, wants to be with me. He leaned into me, almost knocking me over. I caught myself with a little giggle.

"You're just a huge soft puppy, aren't you? I put my arm around his massive neck and took a deep breath, breathing him in, then said, "We'd better go in. I really wish I could have gotten a picture of the two of us together, but we'll have to hold on to the memories once you're human again. Well, come on, big guy, let's go in."

Chapter 13

I stood in the center of a stone circle with Wahaya—a huge, hulking dogman on my right, and Alex on my left. My aunt, Shana, and Adohi were standing on the outer part of the circle with Bidziil, Tsali, and the Elder Okon in a circle between them and us.

The fireplace roared with an eeriness I wasn't prepared for while candles glowed all around us. In between each human circle, there was a circle of stones with a type of rune or sigil carved on them. Surrounding Wahaya, Alex, and me were even larger stones with symbols written in blood. I wasn't sure where they got the blood, but I wasn't going to ask. It was enough that I couldn't stop wondering where the stones came from.

Elder Okon moved in front of me, said some ceremonial words, made some hand gestures, and then handed me a beautiful ceremonial blade. Then he made some more hand gestures toward Wahaya, which was my sign to make a cut in his paw. Which was hard for me to do, but I leaned forward, kissed his paw, and then made the cut. He didn't even flinch, but I did.

Then Elder Okon did the full ceremonial process again, except this time it was directed to Alex. I cut his palm, the same as I had done with Wahaya—I don't know why I kissed their palms before the cuts, but I did. I think it hurt me more to do it than to have my palms cut. Now it was my turn.

Now, both Wahaya and Alex had blood dripping from their cuts, and it was being gathered in wooden bowls in front of them. Then Elder Okon moved back to me and took the ceremonial blade. He said a few words in his chant, then he slit both of my palms. I flinched but didn't scream, even though I felt like it. Tears welled up, and a few slipped down my cheek. I heard both Wahaya and Alex growl when I flinched.

Then he took my right hand and bound it to Wahaya, and my left hand and bound it to Alex. Cut to cut. I pulled both of them to me and placed our hands on my chest near my heart. Both of them encircled me, bringing us together.

As we stood there, our blood mixed, the bond growing stronger between the three of us, and Okon began a new chant. First, the inner ring began chanting. Then those on the outer ring, and then it was time for the three of us to repeat the words of the chant. I began, then Wahaya joined, and, lastly, Alex. Wahaya's words were growled, but they were understandable even in his dogman form. They were clear to me because even though he spoke out loud, he also spoke in my mind.

After our portion of the ritual was completed, the third round, Elder Okon, Tsali, and Bidziil said a few final words, and I noticed that the outer circle had stopped. Then, before I realized what was going on, both Wahaya and Alex collapsed, dragging me down with them since we were bound together, and I refused to let go of their hands.

As they collapsed, the candles went out, and the fire in the fireplace turned blood red, then shot up before extinguishing on its own. Bidziil ran and turned on the lights as Tsali and Elder Okon came to cut the ties binding the three of us together. He then checked the pulse of both the man and the creature. He looked up at me with a solemn look, shook his head, and said, "Wahaya is gone, and Alex's pulse is extremely faint."

I felt numb at his words. Tears flowed as I tried pulling both of them to me. Through the blur of tears, I noticed that a symbol was forming on both of their chests. I clung to them as best I could, not wanting to believe that Wahaya was gone, and Alex was barely there.

Tsali worked to pull me away from them, "We need to get him to the couch. Then we must wait to see if the ceremony worked."

Bidziil and Elder Okon came over, and the three of them moved Alex to the couch. I clung to Wahaya, his fur growing wet from my tears. Wahaya transformed in front of us into his human form. But when they went to move his body, it evaporated into thin air right out of our hands. At that moment—I *lost* it.

I couldn't hold back the storm of tears and astonishment at what had just happened. I turned back to Alex and saw his face was scrunched in pain. I noticed the symbol on his chest was getting brighter, as if it were being burned with a branding iron, and deeper than just his skin. I went to him, but he moaned from the pain when I tried to touch it. Not sure why I tried to touch it—I jerked my hand back, but at least I knew he was still alive. Barely, but still alive. I leaned over and kissed him.

All of a sudden, from upstairs, we heard banging, howls, and Mark yelling for someone to come up and help him. Shana ran past Tsali and me. We were trying to make Alex as comfortable as possible. Adohi slowly worked his way behind everyone, though he was still on crutches. Tsali told me to please calm down and to stay and help Alex while he went upstairs with the others to see what was going on. He also asked me to try and get the fire and candles relit for the next ceremony, which he hoped would take place as soon as possible. They first had to make sure we were all safe so they could focus. He promised he wouldn't leave us alone for long.

The basement felt empty and cold without Wahaya and Alex. Alex was barely hanging on. Was I really worth their lives? But I couldn't think about that now; there were things to do.

I was able to get all the candles and the fireplace relit. Although it took a bit of work, it finally roared to full height. Just as the fire steadied, there was scratching at the back door. I got down on all fours and crawled over to stay out of the line of the windows. Though they were small and only a few, I wanted to stay hidden. I had to make sure the door and shutters were locked and bolted. I peeked out the door's shade to see a huge ass dogman standing there, almost as big as Wahaya was. I guess they sensed he wasn't around to protect us anymore. Thankfully, it didn't catch me looking out. I slowly moved back to be near Alex. He was breathing shallowly... but he was breathing. He seemed to be in some sort of coma.

Time seemed to stand still, but eventually Tsali, Bidziil, and Elder Okon came back downstairs to start on the next phase of ceremonies. Tsali came over to check on Alex, saying, "Things have calmed down for the moment. We are starting the ritual as soon as I can get things set up. But they will need your help upstairs. I will take care of Alex before starting the ritual. I have a feeling he will come through okay."

Not wanting to leave him, I hesitated before standing to leave, "Tsali, there was one of the dogmen at the door. It was scratching on the frame, so I made sure everything was locked up, and I made sure the bars on the door were still secure." I quickly gave him an update on Alex, then he thanked me and got started putting things together for the next ritual phase of the ceremony.

Before I left, I kissed Alex—Wahaya—or maybe both. I softly whispered against his lips, "I promise you I'll be back, but you need to be here waiting for me. I love both of you, and now that we have found each other, you'd better be here *and* awake." I kissed him one more time, then went up the stairs, saying a silent prayer on the way and hoping that one of them was in there and could hear me.

Once upstairs, I saw Aunt Ulla and Shana in the kitchen making coffee and a few snacks. I walked through to the dining room and found Mark loading rifles and a few shotguns with ammo. He glanced up, but there was a dark look of fear on his face I'd never seen before.

"How's Alex?" he asked, "Things were so crazy I didn't get a chance to ask the others. Did the ceremony work?"

I couldn't hide my concern, "I don't know, the ritual part seemed to go well, but... umm, they both passed out. A symbol appeared on their chests and then Wahaya... faded into nothing." Tears pricked my eyes remembering when they both passed out and then Wahaya... now he was gone, and Alex...

Trying to hold back more tears and with a quiver in my voice, "I'm sorry... umm, Alex's in some sort of coma. I wanted to stay, but Tsali said you needed help up here and they're getting ready for the next ritual of the final ceremony, so he told me to come up and help however I can."

Before either of us could say another word, there was a loud knock at the front door. Both of us grabbed a shotgun and ran over. He motioned for me to get behind him as we both looked out the window. There, on the doorstep, standing as if nothing strange was going on, was Richard Jackson Skullthorn. All pompous and arrogant. I didn't know what came over me, but I grabbed the door and flung it open, shouting, "What the *hell* do you want?"

I'd caught Mark off guard by running out, but he caught up and stood by me. Mr. Skullthorn tried to push past us as if he owned the place. Mark stepped in front of him, blocking him, so he yelled around Mark, "Excuse me, but I want to talk to your aunt. Ursula! Where are you? We have business to discuss," his voice rang out in a sickening sing-songy way.

Aunt Ulla came out of the kitchen like a rocket, "What the hell do you want, Skullthorn? We don't have any business to discuss, and I want you out of my home, now!"

"Oh, don't be like that, Ursula. Surely, we can talk business, or you all can keep fighting my little *pets*—the big, bad dogmen. *When* you sell me this place, I'll even give you, oh... thirty grand."

"Skullthorn, I already told you over and over, nothing you offer me will be good enough for me to sell to you. Now leave, or I might accidentally fall on a shotgun and set it off in your direction."

Mr. Skullthorn turned, and I stepped forward to shut the door behind him, but he quickly grabbed me, causing me to drop the shotgun and giving him a larger opening to pull me through the door and shut it behind us.

Both creatures were outside waiting for him. One held the door as Mark tried to open it, then Skullthorn pushed me to the other creature, which threw me over its shoulder and took off running. Skullthorn got in his truck, and the one holding the door jumped in the back, and they took off. I could hear Mark, my aunt, and Shana all yelling for me as the dogman carried me into the woods.

Screaming and beating the creature's back was only hurting my hands. He wasn't even fazed. He just kept running as if I were a feather instead of a woman who weighed a hundred and forty pounds. As he was running through the woods, and I bounced against his stinky, hairy back, I started thinking strange thoughts.

Why had we done the Soul Rejoining ritual first? I could use Wahaya's help right now... and even Alex couldn't help Mark find me. No one even knows how long he'd be in a coma. Crap—what can I do to get this thing to put me down without killing me?

"Put me down—you stink!" I yelled. "You smell worse than a dead skunk on the side of a road on a hot summer day! Damn it, put me down!" I kept beating his back with my fists, hoping to loosen his grip. Which didn't happen, it only hurt my hands more, but I got a snicker out of him.

After what seemed like forever of the dogman running at a full sprint, we were so high up the mountain that I was starting to have issues breathing. He began to slow down to a walk and growled out in understandable English, "Boss man gave you to me. Your mate is gone, you mine now. I watched you mate him, so it's possible."

He ran his clawed hand up the inside of my thighs, and I cringed. I tried to wiggle out of his grip without any success. I didn't think I had ever been so scared in my life, not even when I first saw Wahaya. Next thing I knew, the other one joined us, and they started squaring off, growling at each other—squaring off to fight, not caring that I was still on its shoulder. I was scared there was going to be a tug-of-war, with me as the thing to tug apart, so I started screaming. All of a sudden, I heard Skullthorn yell at them to stop fighting. He pushed a button on some sort of device as he shot into the air, and they immediately stopped. I was dropped at Skullthorn's feet.

Skullthorn smirked as he looked down at me. I had never seen any living human look so evil before in my whole life.

"Since you seem to like dogmen," he started, "I thought these two could share you for a little while—whether your aunt decides to sell or not. If your aunt does sell me her property, I might let you go. She will either sell to me, or I will make sure you will end up as a chew toy for my two friends here. We will give her one hour to stew, then I'll contact her. Ultimatums have a way of working out when there is leverage. Until then I wouldn't do anything too stupid, or they might not wait for my permission."

Chapter 14

Mark

I watched as Shana paced and bit her nails. Then she turned to me and yelled, "Mark, what are we going to do? We can't sit here and wait—they'll kill her!"

"Shana, I'm pretty sure he has a plan," I replied. "He'll want to use her as leverage to get Aunt Ulla to sell. He won't let them kill her, at least not yet, because if she's dead, then that would definitely put a kink in any plan he may have concocted. We have to be smart about this. Keep her alive while making sure he doesn't get what he wants."

Aunt Ulla stood up and joined Shana in pacing. Then, she took a deep breath as she wiped away a few tears and said, "You're right Mark... we need to handle this in a smart way, but we also need to get her back *now*. What if one of those *monsters* decides she looks tasty, or Skullthorn loses control? Oh my God, the ritual. Mark, please!"

Realizing what Aunt Ulla had just said, I took off for the basement with Shana right on my heels. Bursting into the room, I yelled, "Tsali, STOP! They took Ashley!"

Tsali, Bidziil, Elder Okon, and Adohi all looked up from their spots on the floor. I tried to explain what happened and that we had to figure out how to rescue Ashley before the ritual was in full force. While talking, I noticed Stephenson lying on the couch in a coma. He looked dead. But I knew I had to hold it together, so I took a deep breath and asked, "How's Stephenson? Is he..."?

Tsali stood, walked over to check his pulse, showing me while telling me at the same time, "He is alive, we keep checking, and time will tell if he, Wahaya, or by some unknown miracle, both, will awaken. But for now, we must figure out how to save Ms. Ashley. While we continue with the ceremony, the timing will be key. We will figure something out, and I will come up to let you know soon. But for now, go back upstairs and keep watch."

Shana, Aunt Ulla, and I headed back upstairs to work on our own plan. Before heading up, I looked over at Stephenson again. I saw my friend lying on the couch, barely breathing, hell, possibly dying, and I don't know what to do. But I knew that Stephenson wouldn't give up, and neither would I. I had to get Ashley back for him... for all of us. I knew she was key to his healing.

Shana sensed my mood—she could see the fear and concern on my face. She interrupted my thoughts with a long hug. She knew saying something like, "Everything will be fine," wouldn't help, and at that moment—it would've felt more like a lie. All we could do was try to come up with a plan and have faith that the Ancients were doing everything they could to help and to protect Ashley.

If only Stephenson would wake up, Ashley would reappear, and Skullthorn would drop dead. But for now, I needed to be strong for Shana and Aunt Ulla. Between the three of us and the Elders, I was sure we could come up with a plan.

~

Ash

I came to aching and in the dark. Lying on what I guessed was a cave floor. I realized I was tied up and gagged as I tried to sit up, but it was awkward. My nose was assaulted by a strange stench every time I tried to take a breath. It was a musky, moldy smell mixed with wet dog, skunk, and some sort of metallic scent. It was so strong that I could taste it through the gag.

Disgusting.

I must have been knocked out and then tied up. I tried loosening the ropes Skullthorn used, but, unfortunately for me, he must have been a Boy Scout because he knew what he was doing with the knots.

I finally managed to sit up and leaned back on the cave wall. I shivered as the dampness seeped through my shirt and jeans. The back of my head hurt, and I saw a dark patch of dark red had dripped down my shirt. I felt panic coming on, so I tried to calm myself by taking slow, deep breaths, but the stench made me choke and cough.

So, that was a bad idea.

As I slid back against the cave, my thoughts started to run rampant. I hoped the others would be okay. I had an idea of what Skullthorn might try, and I was just as worried about them as I was for myself. Right now, things seem a bit hopeless.

How in the world did I get into this mess?

I started thinking about the past several months and, especially, this last week. It was like I was watching a movie. I had tried to figure out if it was a romance, horror, or, hell, a comedy of horrors. I was thinking it was more of a romantic horror at this point.

Then the question I'd been asking myself reared its head again. How could I fall in love with two men and in such an extremely short amount of time? Well, a half-creature, half-man, in such an extremely short time. I always thought relationships had to move slow—dating, getting to know someone. But with both Wahaya and Alex, it was as if I'd known them all our lives. It was weird to me how I felt closer to Wahaya and Alex in a matter of days than I ever did Richard or anyone else I'd ever been with. Then that one question popped in… was I worth their lives? They thought so. Right now, I would rather have both of them and figure out how to work things, than not to have them at all.

Wow, here I am, in danger, and my mind takes me down a strange rabbit hole. I think my coping mechanism is slightly wonky.

After laughing at myself, I remembered that I had to try to save myself before the hour was up. I was praying I hadn't been out that long and there was still time left. My mind shifted to wondering if, since Wahaya faded away, that meant he was in his dream form, or if he was joined with Alex, or was gone completely.

Maybe calling out to him or Alex could help… it definitely couldn't hurt.

The meditation Tsali had explained to me on how to call out to Wahaya came to mind. I closed my eyes and imagined what the two men looked like, how they felt, smelled, and the taste of their kisses, and I began calling to them. I could feel myself rocking and swaying, adding movement to the chant that I had created.

Suddenly, I felt a presence near me…

My eyes flew open, and if I hadn't been sitting, I would have fallen over. My eyes and mouth were open wide in disbelief. Standing in front of me was my Uncle Carl, who had been dead for about ten years.

I tried to speak through my shock, only to have him shake his head and place his finger to his lips, signaling for me to be quiet.

"Honey," he whispered, "Wahaya and Alex cannot come to you yet. They're both in a liminal state of merging. Their souls are rejoined, and that takes time. The ancestors sent me to help you. Your aunt, Shana, and Mark are trying to come up with a plan to save you—but Skullthorn is an evil man. He has a hold on the other dogmen, and it must be broken first. He plans to have them kill all of you regardless of whether your aunt sells or not. Of course, once dogmen kill you and those at the lodge, he will kill them and take the credit for killing the creatures. He will also get the lodge and land at that point. The Elders and Ancient Spirits are working hard on the ritual portion of the ceremony. It all must be timed perfectly, because when that hold breaks, the creatures will turn on him. *You need to be gone.* I've loosened your ties as much as I could, but it should be enough to help you get out of them. Hurry up and follow me, *don't* make a sound, and do *exactly* what I tell you, no matter what, okay, kiddo?"

I nodded my head and followed his instructions. I was able to wiggle out of the ropes. I didn't know a ghost could actually affect solid things, but he did, and I was grateful. I wiggled out of the ones on my wrists, then untied the ones around my knees and ankles. I stood up slowly since I felt as if I had been beaten and thrown under a moving truck.

My uncle's spirit walked in front of me, letting me know when to stop or speed up, and he helped me wind my way through the cave passages. All of a sudden, he stopped. If he had been real, I would have run right into him. Instead, I went through him. I backed up to look at him as he whispered, "Skullthorn and the creatures are closer to the opening than earlier; we need to go back and take a different tunnel."

He immediately turned and led me down another tunnel to the left that I hadn't even noticed. Good thing I wasn't trying to do this myself, I'd die after being lost in here. Once we made it to the opening, he went out and motioned for me to follow him. We snuck down the side of the mountain toward the lodge—at least, I hoped it was toward the lodge.

Uncle Carl stopped for a brief moment, closed his eyes, nodded, and then pointed out a path he wanted me to take, "Stay low, but move fast. This should take you back to the lodge. Please, hurry! Tsali just let me know they are close to breaking the connection between Skullthorn and the dogmen. Once the link is severed, Tsali, Bidziil, and the Ancients will be working to call them back to their sleep state, or they will have to be destroyed. But you must be away from here, regardless. Go, quietly, and I'll try to keep them off your trail if they realize what's happening. Now go!"

I smiled at my uncle and started to say something, but he began to fade, just like Wahaya used to. As he faded, I felt scared and alone. My senses were on high alert, so every tiny sound sent a bolt of fear racing through my system. I began to slowly make my way down the mountain path he'd pointed out. I knew the dogman had brought me pretty high up, but now that I had to go down on my own, I realized just how far they had taken me. At one point, I slid quite a way down. It hurt like hell, and I could feel every cut as snow-covered rocks and branches tore through my clothes. I was soaked from sliding through the wet snow, but it was faster than my walking pace would have been. I tumbled a few times, adding cuts to my head and giving me a headache.

Time was moving strangely for me. Things seemed to be moving fast as I was hurrying down the mountain, but it also felt like it was taking forever to reach the lodge.

Finally, I could see the roof of it. Just knowing I was almost there gave me the energy I needed to run the rest of the way, no matter the pain. I made it to the driveway of the lodge and started screaming for Mark and Shana. The front door flew open with Shana, Mark, and Aunt Ulla running out. They looked worried, and then Mark raised his shotgun to shoot at something behind me. Shana and Aunt Ulla helped me get inside, then Shana picked up a rifle and went to join Mark. They were shooting round after round until they both ran into the house and bolted the door.

No sooner did we get the door closed and make it a few steps away, when something hit it *hard*. We heard growling coming from outside. Apparently, one of the dogmen had noticed I was gone and found my trail of blood. I guess I had a large enough head start that it gave me time to get away, and with Uncle Carl's help, too, I'm sure.

Mark told us to get to the basement and help the others with the ritual, and he would hold off the dogmen. He began reloading the guns, and we knew he wasn't messing around. Mark used a large caliber, hollow-point ammo that could take down Bigfoot.

Well, shit, I guess bigfoots could be possible too.

I hesitated too long thinking about other things that could exist, so Shana grabbed my arm and began pulling me toward the basement stairs.

"Once we're safely downstairs, I'll check you over and see how bad your wounds are," Shana said.

I looked down at the spot on my shirt and noticed the blood was fresh, then realized the pain I was in. An image of Uncle Carl flashed through my mind, and I shook my head, "No, Uncle Carl said we have to help Tsali strengthen the ritual energy immediately. I'll be fine, I promise. We don't have time to wait."

She shot me a worried look. We stumbled our way down the steps and tried to ignore the angry noises coming from outside. Mark had positioned himself behind us at the top of the stairs so he could see everything and not be ambushed.

Once we made it to the basement, we were able to join in on the second ritual almost immediately. The air was filled with electricity, and the chant was easy enough to pick up on. Aunt Ulla, who had made it down a minute before us, was already in some sort of trance. Shana and I joined in, but I couldn't stop myself from looking over at Alex. He still laid in the same spot on the couch, now covered with a blanket for warmth, but he looked no different than he did after the Soul Rejoining ceremony. I longed to go to him, to let him know I was there—except, I knew all of us were needed. The ritual had to be strong and powerful or it wouldn't work. The Ancients needed all of us to put every ounce of energy we had into it or else this could fail, then it wouldn't matter because we would all be dead.

I closed my eyes and began to chant while pushing out of my mind the sight of Alex on the couch. Along with memories of Wahaya disappearing and the knowing that Mark was upstairs risking his life trying to keep us safe. Slowly, the magic took over my senses, and the feeling of being wrapped in a warm blanket lulled me into an altered transcendental state.

I joined with the others and the Ancient Spirits.

I wasn't sure how I was able to see everything, but we were all in a circle around a large bonfire. Tsali, Okon, Bidziil, Adoni, Aunt Ulla, Shana, and I were joined by Uncle Carl and by what seemed to be a hundred or more Ancient Spirits. All of us were chanting in unison while the surroundings looked and felt as if they were breathing.

The fire began to grow, and in the center of it was a vision of Skullthorn and the two dogmen. It was evident that whatever device he'd used to control them had been broken, and lay in pieces at his feet. He was shooting at them with his handgun, but all it did was anger them. One attacked him, knocking him over, and then they both started tearing him apart. Skullthorn tried to fight back all the way until the end, but he now lay dead with both dogmen still in a frenzy, tearing him apart.

I recognized the area where they were—it was slightly up the mountain outside the lodge. I was in shock at the sight but kept chanting with the others as the energy of the ritual escalated, and I could feel the power surging. I knew we weren't done by any means, and I gave as much power and energy as possible. I stayed glued to the scene in the fire.

The two dogmen stood, turned to one another, roared, and then it was as if the fire consumed them in one surge, and then they were gone.

Chapter 15

I groaned as I tried to sit up, only to have two hands guide me back down.

"Ashley, you need to rest. We stitched up some of your cuts and bandaged the others. You also had a bad head injury. All you need to do now is rest," I heard Shana say as I drifted off again.

~

I opened my eyes to find myself in the clearing where I'd first officially talked to Wahaya. There, standing in front of me, was my uncle.

"Ash, sweetie, I can't thoroughly express how pleased the Ancients are with everyone, and especially you. We were able to end some of the evil that has been destroying the mountain and its people for the last two hundred years. The evil that took me from you, your mom, and Ursula is now gone. It was never proven—but I know that Skullthorn had someone run me off the road; it wasn't the storm or a heart attack that caused the accident. But that's over now. The Ancients wanted you to know that you are one of us—an Elder for the new generation. With you and Ihoki, our mountain will be safe for generations to come."

I looked at my uncle in confusion, "How am I one of you? Am I dead? And who's Ihoki?"

"No, dear child, you are not dead. Only resting from your injuries and all the energy loss from the ceremony. It seems you are quite powerful and helped supercharge the ritual. Your love for them is fierce; it fueled their soul rejoining. We were all focused on putting the other dogmen back into their eternal slumber. But your focus was to save both Wahaya and

Alex. Ihoki is Wahaya and Alex, together. Ihoki means 'he who is powerful.' You will see Alex, but some of his features have been altered, like his eyes. Also, the traits of Wahaya will still be visible too. You may still call him Alex, but to the Ancients and the mountain people—he is Ihoki. When you are ready and rested, you will awaken and rejoin your mate."

I wanted to make sure I was able to say at least a few of the many thoughts running through my head, so I blurted out, "Uncle Carl, am I the reincarnation of Wahaya's wife? And is that why there was such a fast connection between us?"

"Yes, you are Ahyoka, his wife and soul's love, reincarnated. That reason sped up the connection, but the two of you were destined to be together. Not only because of that, but also because of the love Alex has had for you since he first dreamt of you during the war. You would appear to him in his dreams and keep him going during the worst times. Be patient, and he will tell you about them one day. For now, rest and enjoy your family and your love."

"Uncle Carl, one last thing—I've missed you. If you happen to see Mom, will you tell her I miss her, too? Oh, and thank you for everything before, and... now."

Uncle Carl walked closer and gave me a huge, loving hug. "We both watch over you and love you so much. Your mother wanted me to let you know that we are both proud of you and that she is thrilled you left the carpenter - she said he was a tool and not a good one. We both want you to be happy. Please tell your aunt I love and miss her so much, but Bidziil is a good man. She has a long life ahead of her and needs to share it with someone who will love her almost as much as I do." He chuckled a little, then smiled, "Seriously though, I just want her to be loved and happy. And remember, neither of you is ever alone."

I hugged him tighter, knowing this was goodbye, "Love you, uncle. And, please, visit if you can."

He smiled and waved as I watched him fade away again.

~

I heard my name being whispered as I slowly began to come out of the deep sleep I'd been lost in. I tried to open my eyes, but it was harder than I'd imagined.

A kiss pressed to my lips sent a jolt of sparks through my body, and I forced my eyes open. The most gorgeous man I had ever seen, or could have dreamt of, sat next to me on my bed. I saw both Wahaya and Alex in his features. His now sky-blue eyes were overflowing with love. In my heart and soul, I knew my destiny was to create a future with this miracle of a man.

He helped me sit up, and I placed my hands on his face, pulling him closer. We kissed tenderly while still filled with fire and longing. I leaned back and looked into his eyes, "Is everyone safe?"

"Yes," he answered, "and the snow has calmed enough that the authorities were able to take Skullthorn's remains away. Everyone has been worried about you."

"I'm fine now," I whispered as I leaned in and kissed him again. I looked into his soulful eyes and asked, "Ihoki?"

"Yes, my angel?"

"I love you!"

He kissed me again, deeply with passion, before he pulled back long enough for his gaze to lock with mine, "Ashley, I love you too. All parts of me love you. I have Wahaya's memories of his past life and his time as a dogman combined with mine... it's strange, and I know I'm different—me but not me... but I feel whole now. That is why the Ancients gave us the name Ihoki. The name consecrates our soul, making it indivisible. Leaning in again, he claimed my lips, whispering, "I love you so much, and you were worth everything we went through to be here."

As our kiss ended, he pulled me in for a hug, at least until I groaned from the ache of my wounds. Quietly, he climbed into the bed beside me, kissed me one more time, then pulled me to his chest.

"Rest, my love, we have a lifetime to live and a mountain to rebuild."

As I drifted off to sleep, I could hear his heartbeat. The rhythm was steady and strong, louder than either Wahaya or Alex alone. But now, I had them both united in Ihoki.

My dangerous desires... finally tied into one.

Epilogue

Shana, does my dress look okay in the back? This train seems to be a lot longer than I remember from when I tried it on."

"Ashley, it's fine, and you look beautiful," Shana replied, "I was just thinking... I can't believe it's been a year since... well, you and Ihoki got together and how all that happened. So much has changed. Aunt Ulla and Bidzill are taking that trip around the world, your photography is getting noticed—like I always knew it would, and it helped us to start our Save Our Mountain organization. So much happened, and then you and Ihoki decided to make your relationship official. I'm so happy for you two! Not to mention that I'm thrilled I'm getting to be your Matron of Honor. You look gorgeous... Ihoki is going to claim you all over again when he sees you walking down the aisle. Except, we need to hurry so you're not late for your own wedding!"

I hugged Shana with tears in my eyes, saying, "I can't believe it either. Each day I wake up and think to pinch myself, if only mentally, to make sure I'm not dreaming. I mean, have you seen my soon-to-be husband? Drop dead gorgeous, intelligent, kind, caring, connected with his ancestors... in ways that are unbelievable, and he loves me. All of him loves me. I can't believe how blessed I am."

I moved over to the full-length mirror one last time before giving the go-ahead for the music to begin. As we walked out to the clearing where the wedding was to take place, Shana turned to give me one last hug before she turned back around.

Now, standing alone, I watched as Shana followed our friends, Sloan and Sierra, down the aisle to wait for me to join them and my love.

Sloan and Sierra drove all the way from Waynesville, NC, to be in the wedding. They were two friends I met this past year on one of my photo shoots, and the four had become close friends. So, here we were. The two of them, now my bridesmaids, and Shana, my maid of honor. I truly was blessed with friends, family, and a good man.

Our timing for the wedding was perfect because Sloan and Sierra were headed to Scotland next week for a long-overdue vacation, and Aunt Ulla and Bidzill just got back from their 8-month trip around the world.

Shana reached her spot at the altar and then looked to me, giving me a smile that said it's time. Smiling back, I stepped forward into the canopy of trees that formed the aisle. I looked to see all our family, friends, and possibly every mountain tribe member turn and watch as I began my walk down the aisle. I glanced at my bridal trio waiting patiently, then to the Elder who was performing the ritual, and then I saw him.

Ihoki was standing next to the Elder, watching me with a huge smile, and his eyes were filled with tears. Our eyes locked, and all I could see as I walked down the aisle was him. The beauty of our surroundings fell away, our guests disappeared, and I didn't even hear the music anymore.

All I saw was him. All I heard was our heartbeat. And all I felt was the love and desire we had for each other.

Memories of our meeting and how Wahaya and Alex became one flashed through my mind with each step. Two into one, even though they were technically in Alex's body, you could still see them both. There was a difference, and Ihoki was both, but not. I could *feel* them both... within the one. When we make love, somehow, it's both of them loving me, caressing me, and I'm overcome with heat-filled passion just thinking of our unions. I must've been blushing because my cheeks felt like they were on fire just thinking of the most recent adventure in the woods. The snow was cold, but it melted just as fast as I did.

Now, at the altar, I faced my past and my future. I breathed in our destiny. I never thought I would be here, but I couldn't see my future anywhere else or with anyone else.

Destiny brought us together, and eternal love bound us beyond the reach of time.

The End

Other Works: in progress:

Dating Die-Sasters

The Hotel of Time

My Scottish Brownie

The Art of Murder

Murder In the Moonlight

Working Tile 1

Working Title 2

~Stay Tuned~

Other Works: published as Dorey Lee

A Moody Dragon with No Name

A Little Witch's Wish

Want to be the first to know about updates?

Sign up for D. L. Nolan's Quarterly Newsletter and Website

Acknowledgments

My support team:

Nick S., my Sweetheart ~ my love. He inspires me, challenges me, and when we have some downtime, he is my gaming buddy (even when he doesn't want to). Thank you for being my cuddle at the end of each day. I love you, Sweetheart.

Kat L, my sister who has inspired me, gives me feedback on crazy ideas, and who, just like me, has a fascination with the paranormal. Thank you.

Goals Group:

Mary D. ~ Norma S. ~ Shana T. ~ Nick S.

Having you four help to keep me accountable has kept me on track and provided my readers with my bi-weekly blog, children's books, and now my Dangerous Desires.

Beta Readers:

You know who you are ~ each of you provided me with great feedback and encouragement. Knowing that you loved my characters and enjoyed their story warms my heart. I greatly appreciated your taking the time to read, comment, and reply to my questionnaire.

My Editor/Formatter/Friend:

Serenity ~ You have been a friend and classmate, and now you are my editor and formatter. You worked with me on both of my children's books and now on my first of many novels. Thank you for your patience, guidance, and for helping me to become a better writer. You are greatly appreciated ~ Thank you.

Finally, to my inner child ~ for never wanting to give up and having a loud voice in my heart.

About the Author

D. L. Nolan, known to her friends as Dorey, has always dreamed of being an author and artist. In high school, she wrote stories about leprechauns and imagined sharing her tales with the world. As time went on, she continued to dabble in writing, only to tuck those pages away in a box. Dorey eventually gave up on those dreams, believing they were gone forever.

Then, in 2019, she joined a Toastmasters club and wrote a speech about a dragon without a name. Afterward, several members asked, "When is your book coming out?" That was the first inspirational kick in the butt she needed.

A few years later, she published her first children's book, The Moody Dragon with No Name. Next came A Little Witch's Wish. She has now published two children's books—with more to come!

Dorey has long dreamed of writing a novel and has several in the early stages. Now, she has finally completed her first novel—Dangerous Desires.

Blending her love of storytelling with her fascination for cryptids and the paranormal, she brings you the first of many paranormal romance novels. Follow Dorey and her creative adventures at creativelyunlimited.com.

She also writes a bi-weekly blog covering topics such as books, travel, health, and the importance of never giving up on your dreams.

D. L. Nolan